SACRIFICING
AYDA

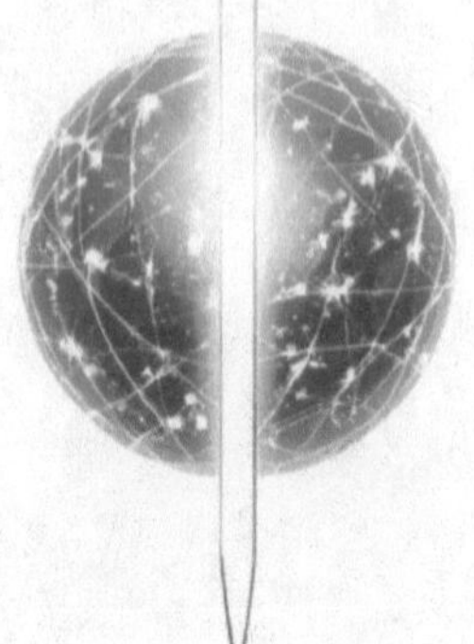

D. A. BEAUMONT

Library of Congress Control Number: 2026908237

Contents

Chapter 1

I crash into my bed as anger gushes through me like a torrent. I want to scream. I want to explode.

"Ayyy-*da!*" Ma calls from the door of our hut. She huffs and bows, trying to catch her breath as she enters our humble home, coming closer and closer to finally catching me. I knew she wouldn't be able to keep up with me, but I had to get out of there. I had to get away from the sanctuary.

Ma finally pushes past the small partition to my 'room,' takes one final deep breath and asks with her voice on edge, "Ayda, what is it *this* time?"

Instead of answering, I push my face deeper into my straw mattress.

"You have to stop this, Ayda," Ma continues. "You can't attack everyone who isn't nice to us. And now I'm going to have to send a peace offering to-"

"No, you don't," I yell into the mattress, "She got what she deserved!"

Back at the sanctuary, I tripped Everly Hughes right as she came out the front doors. No one saw me do it - I should have gotten away clean - but Ma knew. She told me to go and apologize. So I ran.

"We're healers, Ayda," Ma says. "We do no harm."

"No," I reply, sitting up for the first time to look her in the face, "*you're* the healer. And everyone hates you for it. They all call us 'witch' behind our backs. I'll never be like you, Ma. Do you hear me? And I'm going to get as far away from here as I can - all the way to...to....to *Witch Marsh* if I have to!"

"*Ayda!*" Ma gasps. "*Don't say that!* Don't say it here. Don't say it anywhere. Do you know how awful it would be if they took you away from me?"

"No!" I scream back. "I don't know! Could it be any worse than our lives now?"

"Yes!" Ma cries. "It could be *so* much worse! We're here together."

"Well," I say. "I don't want to be here. And I guess that means I don't want to be with *you*."

I push past Ma and rush out of our hut and into the woods. I've had enough of my life in Kern - of going to the schoolhouse every day to endure taunts and jeers. Kat's my only friend, mainly because she doesn't know who her father is - like me - which also makes her an outcast. But she doesn't have the added pressure of being the daughter of someone everyone thinks is a witch. If not for Kat, maybe I really *would* have run off to Witch Marsh by now.

And so in my angst and anger, I wander the woods aimlessly, realizing glumly that I have nowhere to go except back, but I can't bring myself to do it yet, so I decided instead to catch my own supper at the creek instead. I take my line and hook out from my hiding place and get to fishing.

As I cast my line, my anger twirls about in my head with each jiggle and joggle of the worm on my hook, and this is how the time passes, one hour to the next. I'm usually pretty good at fishing, but perhaps today my luck has run out. I won't completely go hungry, though. I can forage some roots - but unfortunately, it's still a bit early in the season for berries.

I look down into the waters and see my reflection - my limp, plain, brown hair. Somehow, I didn't inherit Ma's flowing raven hair. Instead, mine is thinner and lighter. Ma says it helps me fit in here - if *that* were possible. I know I'm not anywhere near as pretty as Kat, who's tall, lanky, graceful, and mild. In fact, I'm not like her at all, even to the point that I sometimes wonder how we're friends.

I'm still caught in these thoughts when I hear footsteps crunching through the woods and intruding on my solitude. They grow nearer and nearer until I find myself looking at one of the oddest-looking boys I have ever laid eyes on. His hair looks like a huge bush of black curls that threatens to cover his whole face at any moment. His darker skin shines a golden-brown, and his clothing is made of some sort of plant fibers I'm not acquainted with (which is unusual since my Ma is an herbalist). And his smile seems like it comes from the very center of him. Right now, it shines at me so brightly that I almost drop my fishing line.

"Hello," the boy says.

I could try to run, but then I would probably have to discard my fishing line.

"Hi," I say, trying to limit the acidity in my voice. "What are you doing here?"

"Someday you will know," the boy replies. "For now, though, let me say that I separated from my traveling companions to take in the beauty of the forest. Now I have come here and met you. I'm Sunny."

"Your name is *Sunny?*" I ask, thinking maybe that it was too much on the nose.

"Yes," he replies. "Will you tell me your name?"

"No," I say. But then, "It's Ayda. Now, if you wouldn't mind, the noise scares the fish away."

"It does?" Sunny asks. "I think you'll find they might bite while we talk anyway."

"Well," I say, trying to think of how else to get rid of this fellow, when my line suddenly goes taut in my hands.

"Would you like some help pulling in your catch?" Sunny asks.

"No," I say resolutely, "I would *not*."

I continue to struggle with the line while this oddly dressed stranger approaches the creek and watches me battle the trout.

"I'm traveling with a delegation from Sandorsville," Sunny says. "It's the year of the Centenary. Did you know that?"

"No," I say, not paying him much attention. Every bit of my focus and effort remains locked on the trout, who seems like he will never tire, and I begin to fear that the line will break until all at once the fish goes limp. Hand over hand I quickly pull onto shore one of the largest trout I've ever seen and smack him with a rock.

"Well, it was nice to meet you, Ayda," Sunny says. "Enjoy your catch." With one more smile, he leaves, trodding off back the way he came, and I try to feel happy about it, but instead I just feel strange.

I clean the trout, make a fire, roast the fish, eat some, and save a fillet for Ma, which I hope will smooth things over when I get home. I pack up and walk back to our hut with a certain amount of fear for what Ma will say when I arrive - something about how I shouldn't run off, or maybe about facing our disagreements, or about working things out. But when I come to our hut, I hear the sound of a horse riding away, and my thoughts about Ma's anger at me leave my head immediately.

"Hey," I say upon entering, "who was that?"

Ma looks up like I've caught her by surprise. Her eyes are puffy and red. Is it from the fumes of the poultice she's mixing?

"Have you been crying?" I ask.

"I have to take this to the Barners," Ma says. "There was an accident."

"Did someone die?"

"No," Ma says, shaking her head.

"Here, I brought this for you," I say, handing her the fish in a cloth. "I caught it."

Ma nods her thanks, squeezes my arm in gratitude, and continues her preparations. "I cleaned your clothes for school tomorrow," she says as she goes to the door. Then she turns back to me. "Families have to stay together - that's the most important thing."

Ma leaves before I have time to reply. Is she trying to guilt me into staying? She's always been very particular about me getting an education, but at the end of the school year, the only way to continue schooling is to go to monastery, which I have no intention of doing (nor would they even extend the invitation). Does she want me to continue studying herbs and healing with her? That's more likely, but I don't want to do that either. I'm leaving - I told her that.

Sometimes I just find Ma so frustrating.

I scowl at the partition that acts as my door, vowing quietly to myself that even if we are physically under the same roof, she and I will not be together for the rest of the evening.

Chapter 2

I'm hardly in a better mood next morning. I squeeze my eyes shut and groan loudly, but there's nothing for it. I pick myself up, quickly dress, then push past Ma without breakfast before I rush down the path towards town.

Leaving Ma behind, though, doesn't help me escape the thunderclouds swirling in my mind, especially as I contemplate the challenges I might face at the schoolhouse. Could there be repercussions for tripping Everly? I know I *thought* I had made a clean getaway but maybe I didn't. And even more concerning, I saw Roland and his crew making eyes at Kat during service yesterday. Like I said, she's pretty, and for some reason that and not knowing who her father is makes her a target for Roland and his gang. Because, while Roland still remembers the last time I kicked him between the legs, he also knows that Kat won't do that. I've talked to her about it, but for some reason she just doesn't seem to have it in her.

When I walk into the school room I quickly look over the seats to see how things are shaping up. We have three groups here – first, there's the Laity, the children of regular working people and farmers who live in town and the surrounding area. Then there are the Cassocks, the children of parents who hold an official role in the Sandorite Ministry; even though only the actual ministers wear cassocks, we use the term to refer to deacons and their children as well. And lastly, there are the undesirables, me and Kat.

I join Kat in the back and sit down. The cassocks walk in loudly next, talking about their ride in. Among their number are Evelyn and Roland, the children of Minister Hightower, and Aden and Devon, both the sons of wealthy deacons. Everly is absent, possibly because I tripped her yesterday. I know Aden somewhat because of all the visits his father makes to our hut for his health issues, but he is over there with them and definitely not over here with us.

"Hey, Kat," Roland whispers as he takes his seat. Miss Culbert doesn't hear as she writes out our lessons on the board. "We've got a little present for you. Show her Devon," Roland says, prompting Devon to pull a large caterpillar from his lunch pail. They all grin like the biggest fools, and Devon quickly hides it under his hand again.

"This is a special caterpillar," Roland says, "isn't it, Devon? If you eat it, you'll turn beautiful like a butterfly."

"She's already pretty, you moron," I whisper in Kat's defense, "prettier than your wife will be. Why don't you save it for her?"

Roland glares at me. "My wife will be ten times prettier than Kat, but there's no magic caterpillar in the world that could help *you*, Ayda Cellars."

I stick my tongue out at him in response.

Kat, somewhat bewildered, gives me a concerned look but says nothing. It's not the first time Roland has preyed on her in this manner. And, as usual, she seems ready to keep her head down and take the brunt of his taunting, whether it's right or not.

"I hear it's delicious too," Roland says, "so you'll have to tell us, Kat, what it tastes like."

"Young Mr. Hightower?" Miss Culbert calls back.

"Oh, I'm just helping Katherine understand today's lesson, Miss Culbert," Roland replies.

"Why, thank you, Roland. You're too kind," Miss Culbert says, turning back to her writing on the board.

"I've tried to tell you that there's no such thing as magic caterpillars," Aden replies in a whisper while Devon catches the caterpillar from walking up his shoulder. "If it really does have some magic properties, we'd be better off trying to crush it and apply it directly to her face."

"She has to eat it," Roland pronounces under his breath.

Now Kat looks like she's going to cry.

"What?" Roland whispers snidely, "You don't want to be pretty? And here we are, willing to do you a favor. You should be thanking me, kitty-kat."

And that's when I cut in. "You touch her at all, Roland Hightower, and I'll shove your face in the mud so hard you'll be blowing brown bubbles out your snotter till seventh day, and then I'll take that caterpillar and shove it so far up your -"

"Ayda Cellars!"

"That butterflies will start -."

"*Ayda! Come here - you come here immediately!*" Miss Culbert bellows in outrage from her gaunt little frame. I stand there dumbly, realizing too late that I shouldn't have raised my voice. Then, with some dramatic huffing and a great air of righteous indignation, Miss Culbert takes the switch from her desk, walks back to where I stand, bends me over right there in front of the class, and gives me my first switching for the week. "And at recess, you'll copy the Holy Writs 50 times. Now sit *down!* And - and keep your *vile* tongue locked behind your teeth, or I'll wash it clean of filth with soap!"

"Soap can't actually wash away vocabulary," Aden says, but Miss Culbert doesn't hear him. He's always been something of a know-it-all, not like Devon, who I've seen eat his own boogers and who lets Roland do all his thinking for him. And then Roland, the king idiot, does whatever he likes without any repercussions. Evelyn merely smiles at her brother's antics. She rarely takes part (unlike the absent Everly, who I assume wants to become the next Mrs. Hightower someday), but she never rebukes him either.

The morning's lesson passes slowly, but not slowly enough, because when our break time comes, I am still directed to remain in my seat and begin copying.

Do right

True sight

Don't lie

No sly

Don't kill

Love still

Don't steal

Wounds heal

Thank be

Remember me

Only 49 more times, and Miss Culbert will release me. I can feel her eyes turning back every few seconds to ensure that I'm doing my penance. She sits there in the doorway with a book in her hand. Whether looking at me or looking at her book, her focus isn't where it should be. I try to glimpse Kat over her shoulder.

My sloppy writing keeps rushing out of me.

Remember me. 35 now, just 15 to go. I glance up again through the window and spy Devon grabbing Kat by the shoulders and hauling her behind the tree where Miss Culbert can't see.

I won't let them do it. Not this time.

I break free from my seat and let my unfinished assignment fall at Miss Culbert's feet as I push past her. I run fast, which was my original sin against Roland Hightower, beating him at foot races when we were first years until they told me I couldn't compete because dirty witches weren't allowed.

Maybe they don't remember my speed – I'm going so fast I can barely hear the words I'm huffing under my breath. I bite through the pain - I'm halfway across the yard as Devon hands the caterpillar over to Roland. They dump Kat on the ground, and Devon holds her down as Aden looks on. Roland's hand starts descending towards Kat's mouth. And that's when my shoulder hits Roland with a loud *snap*.

I fall back, jarred and disoriented. I feel pain too, but I can't place it, and I eventually shake myself off and get up from the ground. Roland tries to scream but produces an odd hissing noise instead, as though his lungs won't work. And then Miss Culbert comes running.

"*Ayda!*"

"If you touch Kat while I'm away," I whisper, bent over Roland, "I'll do exactly what I said I would."

As I look over Roland's fallen body, though, I consider that maybe he won't be able to attack Kat in my absence anyway. Then my ear explodes in pain as Miss Culbert yanks me up by it so hard that I wonder if my lobe might come off. Now her face is right in mine, but she doesn't address me.

"Aden," Miss Culbert says. "Run for the doctor. Hurry." Without a second glance, he runs over to the horse pen, mounts, and rides off. I stay put, my earlobe pained, smelling Miss Culbert's breath. I wait, gritting my teeth. Her hand suddenly slaps me so hard across the face that I think I see a light for a moment. I can't be sure, though, because before I know it, I'm being marched back to the schoolroom.

"Miss Culbert, but Miss Culbert!" I protest as she pulls me along. "Roland, he -"

"I'm not addressing Roland's behavior at the moment, am I?" Miss Culbert says, still dragging me. "In fact, he's in no condition for it, is he? - *Is he?*"

"But, but..."

The Hightowers are untouchable. I shouldn't have bothered with my protest.

Even thinking of the switch seems to make it materialize in Miss Culbert's hand before she pulls me out of the schoolhouse and around to the side with the most bushes for privacy.

"I hoped, Miss Cellars, that your thirteenth birthday last week would in some way indicate your growing maturity, but how woefully mistaken I was! Now bend over and pull down your britches."

Bare skin. I grit my teeth.

"And what's even worse," Miss Culbert cries, "I don't think you're repentant at all!"

I don't reply. Instead, I bend over and brace myself against an old, knotted bush.

As the switch lands for its first strike, my mind goes somewhere else. It retreats from the pain to a place I keep just for moments like these. In that place, I'm escaping from Kern. I know there's no way Miss Culbert will recommend me to continue my education once I've aged out at the end of this year. I'll finally leave this miserable parish and never look back. I'll travel east to one of the logging camps in Fenton's Wood. It's east of Bayton. In fact, it's the easternmost city in Zandria. That's been my plan for a while.

Switch.

Ma will be disappointed that learning to read didn't make a bigger difference in my life. But it's my life, not hers. Maybe Kat will come with me and escape her fate here as well. Maybe life can be something else besides this if I can just get away. Maybe I'll go even farther than that...

Switch.

Because I have a secret, they called me a witch all those years. And then I found a little book. It scared me at first. But over the last year, with every insult and wrong, I became more and more willing to read it.

Switch.

Witch Marsh. I could go all the way to Witch Marsh. I haven't even told Kat about this new plan. But I've become certain that it's my true home. That's who they think I am. That's who they're so afraid of. Then maybe I'll come back here someday - after I've learned everything I can there. Then maybe they'll be sorry. Then maybe they'll wish they were nicer to me, wish they had stuck up for me.

Switch.

Miss Culbert's arm tires and her last blow barely lands with a thump, but I'm so caught up in my own thoughts that I barely realize she's stopped.

"*Now*," Miss Culbert says breathily, looking at the bruises of her handiwork before standing back in satisfaction. "I have no choice but to submit a report to Minister Hightower. It's his son, so there's no avoiding it. Miss Cellars?"

I look up at Miss Culbert, hiding my backside gingerly back in my britches and dress.

"Do you have anything to say for yourself?" She looks at me so expectantly that I am a little unnerved by it. "Anything at all?"

I stare at her uncomprehendingly.

"You know, don't you, that the Centenary is almost upon us?"

I nod, not really comprehending, just nodding to be through with it.

"Nothing?" she asks.

I think for a moment, trying to grasp what she could possibly mean, but in the end, I shake my head.

"*Go*," she says forcefully. "Just *go*."

"When do you want me to come back?" I ask. I've been suspended before, and it's always measured in days.

"Don't worry about it," Miss Culbert says, shaking her head. "I'll...I'll let you know after I confer with Minister Hightower." She almost looks apologetic as I continue to stare at her until her expression reverts to anger. "*Go!*"

I'm shaken. What will happen to me if Roland's injuries are worse than I thought? What will happen to me if he dies?

Chapter 3

When I wake up the following morning, Ma's already up and mixing a concoction of herbs above a fire. I, of course, never told Ma last night about what happened at school, and if I can help it, she'll never know. I'll hide in the woods during school time until I'm told I can return, and since Miss Culbert never comes out to our little hovel by the woods - and in fact, she regularly calls Ma's remedies both witchcraft and sacrilege in my hearing - and since Ma only goes into town when absolutely necessary, I doubt she will ever learn of my latest transgression, or any of the others.

Ma cooks an egg in a pan for me when I come out of my room. She folds it over, scoops it up, and deposits it on a plate before handing it to me. "I know we talked about having Kat over tonight," she says to me, "but with the lot falling on Kern for the Centenary, I think she'll be too busy in the tavern with her mother. All sorts of guests are coming from all over Zandria."

"*Wait*," I say. I had forgotten about having Kat over. But also - "Miss Culbert mentioned the centenary yesterday."

"As well she might," Ma says, sitting me down with a fork. "She likely has several students in the drawing for the sacrifice - a few current and several past students. You'll be in the lottery too. You might have dodged it if your birthday were next week instead of last week, but don't you worry. There must be a hundred young folks between the ages of thirteen and sixteen in the parish working the fields, apprenticing in town, and studying with the Minister to take their exams for monastery."

"Right," I say, thinking about Miss Culbert yesterday. Why had she brought up the Centenary to me? It was almost as though...

"The Centenary Sacrifice is chosen randomly, right?" I ask.

"Of course," Ma says.

An uneasy feeling settles over me.

"I've got to get to school, Ma," I say, handing back the plate.

"Of course, dear. And I'm sorry about Kat coming over. But you can ask her if she can still make it."

"Right," I say, pushing the rest of the egg into my mouth. "I've got to go!"

"Don't you want your lunch?" Ma calls after me.

"No!" I call back as I race along the path towards Kern.

The centenary sacrifice, I think, looping the phrase in my mind over and over again. What do I remember about it? Anything? Am I worrying for nothing? But the look in Miss Culbert's eyes - it freezes my heart just remembering it.

I'm not paying attention to what's coming around the bend.

"Neeeeeiiiiigh!" BAM!

I find myself lying in the path with a horse reared high above me. Its rider slides off backwards and falls behind its tail. I roll before hooves come thundering down to crush me, but my shoulder still feels sore as I scramble to my feet.

"Deacon Jeffries!" I cry, right as Aden rides up behind his father. What is this cassock doing on the path to our hut?

"Are you alright?" the deacon asks as he struggles to get to his feet. He's a well-built, sturdy man, known for his large estate north of Kern, but now he hobbles like his ankle is injured. "Come back here. You may be injured," he calls. "Your mother should take a look at you."

"I'm *fine*," I shout, shaking him away from me. The last thing I need is a cassock giving me advice.

"I've got to go!" I call behind myself as I hurry along.

"Wait!" he calls.

I glance at Aden as I rush by. Did he tell his father about yesterday? Of course he did.

"I'll be late to school!" I cry as I run. This time, I try to make sure that I keep an eye out for anyone coming down our path. I hear Deacon Jeffries calling after me, but I ignore him. After a few moments, though, I hear another rider now coming up behind me, and Aden trots up next to me.

"What do you want?" I ask.

"Just making sure you're alright," Aden says. "And...I thought you might want to know that Roland is all right. They say he's actually doing much better."

"He is?" I say, feeling relief for the first time today. I even slow down a little and let Aden ride next to me.

"Do you know anything about this Centenary, Aden?" I ask.

"Well, firstly, it's held every hundred years," he replies.

"I know *that*," I say. "I mean, about the sacrifice? What's the story again?...you know, about the centenary...?"

"But you've heard Minister Hightower's sermons," Aden says. "He's spoken on it several times."

Actually, I have become quite adept at tuning out the Minister's long-winded and monotonous sermons that drone on and on, but all I say to Aden is, "Of course I heard them, but I want to hear it again - from *you*."

"Well," Aden says, "Sandor made Landria and everything else - that's how it begins. He pulled it out of the sea - something like that. Then he made people, and then put us all on the island. And he lived here on the island with us and went walking with us every morning until Notso fell from the sky and made that big old crater in the center of the island. And the people of Landria were curious, so they went down into the crater and talked to him, and he said to Father and Mother, 'Is it not so that Sandor has told you that if you walk with him every day, you will have all you ever need and will never know pain, suffering, and death?'

And Mother said, 'Sandor said it so.'

And Notso replied, 'He says this because he knows that if you walk with me, I will share with you the beautiful riches of this crater and will show you how to wield great power, and you will become great in this land. You will then know all the wonderful things I can teach you that Sandor wishes to keep from you. Can you not see that this is so?'

And Father, who Sandor had taught True Sight, saw that this was so.

So in the morning, Father and Mother hid themselves from Sandor and presented themselves to Notso to walk with him instead. But Sandor appeared to them just as they were about to set out.

'What is this that you have done?' Sandor asked.

'We have come to go walking with this one," Father replied, pointing to Notso.

'Since you have chosen him over me,' Sandor said, 'you will walk with him, and you will know pain, suffering, and death."

"But Notso will share riches with us and teach us wonderful things," Father and Mother said.

"He will only share with you those things which are not, and you will know pain, suffering, and death," Sandor said. "But I will not allow him to rule over you without restraint. I will bind him to the place where he fell. And in the hundredth year, you will hold a Centenary for the price of your transgression to be paid in blood. And the Wilder will come to guide the sacrifice in the hundredth year.'

And one hundred years after that, one of our Great Parents' great-grand-children, Shana, became the first sacrifice to Notso. And the sacrifice has been made every hundred years since that day."

I nod. All the elements are familiar to me, but I feel like I'm hearing them now with new ears. But there's one thing I feel is left out. "How," I say slowly, "how does the centenary die?"

"Well," Aden says, "there's an altar...for sacrifice. I don't know anything more specific about that."

If Aden doesn't know anything else, I don't know who would. He's raised his hand for every question our teacher has asked the class ever since we started at lower school.

"Are you worried? I'll be in the drawing too. In fact, my birthday was pretty recent.""You will be?" I ask.

"By the way - where are you going? Everyone knows you've been sus-pended."

"Everyone except my Ma," I say, swallowing hard, "but I guess your Da will fix that, won't he?"

"Probably," Aden says. "He said he wanted to warn your Ma away from coming into town for the next few days. The officials from Sandorsville will be here, and you know how they don't take well to people in your Ma's profession. But my Da's been getting tinctures from your Ma my whole life, so he tries to look out for her."

I nod, trying to think back to the times I have seen Mr. Jeffries come by. Usually, I'm in school. The thing about it is, parish folk call Ma a witch until they get sick - and then they pay her whatever she asks.

"Where will you go today?" Aden asks.

I shake my head. "I need to talk to Miss Culbert about how long I'll be out of school. After that...?"

I'm a little surprised at how quickly my relationship with Aden comes back. We played as children, I suppose, when his Da was coming over for his tinctures for back pain. It almost feels...nice, but I try to crush this feeling and shove it deep down inside of me.

I walk, and he rides the rest of the way to the schoolhouse in silence. I watch the people of Kern's eyes fall on me. All they see is the daughter of a witch. Across the Jaggar mountains lies a whole nation of witches, ones who fought Zandria in a war, but that was hundreds of years ago. Some ignorant people say Ma moved here from Witch Marsh, but she actually came from Fishton in Western Zandria, nowhere near Witch Marsh, and her uncle even visited us from there. But people don't care much about evidence. Not when they want to be angry at you. It's their anger that they care about.

"Kat!" I call when I see her near the schoolhouse door. She runs and hugs me. She's tall. Supposedly, her father is from the whistling cliffs, where everyone is supposed to be seven feet.

"You're not thirteen until the sixth month, right?" I ask, and she shakes her head 'no.'

"They're here," Kat says. "They're here right now to cast the lot!"

I rush to the schoolroom door and take in all the cossacks standing up near the board with Miss Culbert. I recognize Minister Hightower, but several others I have never seen, including a man in red vestments who reaches into a bowl, swirls his hand around, and raises out a piece of paper before pronouncing, "It is with great joy that I declare Ayda Cellars as our next Centenary Sacrifice!" He says it with so much excitement that he might be announcing a prize mutton dinner rather than my impending death. Miss Culbert looks straight into my eyes and gives me a small and knowing smile.

Chapter 4

I run.

I don't think about it. I'm just standing there one moment, and the next I'm sprinting back to town. I don't think about anything else - breathe - run - breathe - run.

I make it all the way to the feed store before the sound of galloping horses finally reaches my ears. I keep running, but the sound grows and grows until the horses trample into the dirt streets. *SMACK*

I'm sent crashing to the ground as the mounted Zandrian Guards thunder by. And when I finally shake myself from the sting of another blow from a horse, my pursuers are already turned back around and galloping towards me again. The riders surround me, dismount, and grab me with their hard gauntleted hands, lifting me to my feet. They inspect their handiwork as I stare back at their tightly pressed uniforms and stony glares.

A few moments pass like this in their ironfisted custody before a series of wagons arrive at our little circle, and the man in red vestments steps out and approaches me.

"Ah, Miss Cellars," he says. "I think you heard my announcement at the school. Congratulations. I'm High Minister Gerald Fry from Sandorsville. I'm here to get you going on your journey to the Pit, but before that, we would love to have you enjoy today's festival as a token of our thanks for your sacrifice."

"My sacrifice?" I ask.

"Yes, your sacrifice," Minister Fry says. "Come along now. You should enjoy the festival. It's in your honor, after all."

I pause for a moment. I could run myself through on one of the guards' swords, but apart from that, I have no choice but to go with them. As they pull me to the carriage, I catch a glimpse of Kat's mother at the tavern door. This pleasant sight is cut off when I am shoved up the carriage steps and into its cabin, where I find Miss Culbert waiting for me.

"It's more appropriate for you to ride with your teacher," High Minister Fry says from the door. "I'll see you at the fair."

I turn back to Miss Culbert as the door closes. Her stern face and eyes don't soften as she meets my gaze.

"It wasn't a mistake," I say, "that I was chosen today, was it?"

Miss Culbert snickers, "Well, we had to pick someone, *didn't we?*"

"That's not what choosing by *lot* means!" I say.

Miss Culbert's sharp, wrinkled face smiles. "You're such a naive girl, Ayda. Do you think we have so many young people to just get rid of anyone? So, of course, they came to me - who else knows all the young people in our parish better than I do? And of course they asked, who can we do without? And if you should blame anyone, you should look squarely at yourself! What did you think would happen when you nearly killed the minister's son the day before the choosing? He wanted to put you in the stocks. Or have you whipped. Or even burned as a witch. But *now*...now you get to save face. You'll be a hero. Your name will go down in history, just like Rollo Barnes from a hundred years ago. They'll be saying your name - Ayda Cellars - when we teach the history of the Centenary. Your life will be short, but was it really going anywhere anyway? You're an outcast. Do you really want another fifty years of that? I feel, in a way, that I've actually done you a favor."

"Should I strangle you in this cab?" I ask, "Would that be a favor? Would I be saving you from miserable years of declining health and your students' disdain?" I pause for effect. "*How could you do this to me?*"

Miss Culbert shrinks away at my words, pushing herself as far away from me as possible in the enclosed space, perhaps fearing that I will make good on my threat of strangulation. For the rest of the carriage ride, she merely shoots me the glare of her beady eyes but says nothing else. When the carriage slows to a stop, she quickly exits, rescuing me from her company. I barge out as well, but find myself strangely in a place humming with activity.

I know I'm at the fairgrounds, but they look quite different from the quaint annually held blossom festivals that our class visited in years past. Besides the addition of many attractions, I also see Sandor's symbol - a walking staff with an eagle's head knob - erected as wooden statues along with a platform and podium.

Booths with flower displays are still present, and I presume there will still be prizes, but there are also vendors of sweet treats that I have only ever heard of by description - and acrobats, and contests of combat, and meat cooked over a fire, and colored streamers and ribbons everywhere. Wealthy men and women in their fine garments sashay from one side of the fair to the other. Only here and there do I see any townspeople I know.

"Esteemed Miss Cellars," Minister Fry says at my shoulder, "we certainly want you to enjoy everything the festival has to offer. We just need to find you the right chaperone. Perhaps your teacher would be willing? Oh no, where has she gone?"

"*I* volunteer," a voice says from somewhere over Minister Fry's shoulder. And there I see again the boy I met in the woods - Sunny - who still stands out amidst all the costumes and chaos of the fair with his golden-brown skin and strange plant fiber attire.

"Hello," Sunny says. "It's good to see you again. I've come to guide you."

"Guide me?" I ask.

"On your quest," he says.

"Do you mean my *sacrifice?*" I reply.

"Your quest of sacrifice," Sunny confirms. "You have been chosen. And no one may be chosen outside of Sandor's will. And I will be with you. You don't have to be afraid."

"Sunny," Mr. Fry says, forcing a smile, "is the Wilder in case you hadn't figured that out. He showed up a couple of months ago and has been with us for this whole process."

"And he knows the way to Notso's Pit?" I ask, "Where am I to be...?"

"...yes," Mr. Fry says. "The Wilders have never let us down. Even the young ones. In fact, it is said that their archipelago is mostly rocky and barren lands, not unlike the mountains and the crater that run through the middle of our island. They are the best traveled there, even better than our mining surveyors, who, as it turns out, won't go too close to the Pit, even for large sums of money."

"It's not a place for the faint of heart," Sunny says.

Minister Fry gives a big belly laugh, shaking his head like this is a wonderful joke. "It's completely safe. For the sacrifice. The one we're obligated to make. Which is a great honor. But just to make sure you get there safely, we intend to give you even more help to find your way. The Wilder, actually, is more of a ceremonial role these days. Now, why don't you two get acquainted? Get yourselves something to eat, watch the performers, and have a good time. Fredrick and Galt will be nearby if you need anything, including some spending money."

The two armed guards appear directly behind us, and Sunny smiles as we start walking through the fair. No obvious escape routes come to mind

I look at him. I have never met anyone quite as strange as Sunny. He pushes his bushy hair out of his face, smiles, and says, "Come on," before leading the way.

After walking past many attractions and vendors, we come to a number of posts driven into the ground, with horses tied to them. The horses graze from a hay trough. Carriages and wagons are parked just beyond there as a man scoops horse dung into a small pit he's dug.

"Horsemaster," Sunny says.

The man turns from his shovel and says, "Most call me Doug."

"Doug," Sunny continues, "we have the High Minister's written consent to take whatever supplies we need for our mission." Sunny pulls a paper from inside his pouch and shows it to Doug.

"Can't read," Doug says.

"Ayda, please read this paper for Doug."

I sigh, look at the paper, and read, "*The High Minister Gerald Fry does hereby give his consent for Sunny of the Wilder people to use any and all resources of the Ministry in order to accomplish his mission as it pertains to the sacrifice of the Centenary.*"

"That will be three horses, please," Sunny says.

"But I've never ridden," I say.

"Don't worry," Sunny replies.

I climb onto the horse with difficulty. My skirt pulls as I try to raise my legs, making it impossible to sit astride it.

"You'll have to sit to the side until we can get you some new clothes," Sunny says. "We'd better go now, though. Fredrick and Galt have found us."

"I thought we had the High Minister's permission," I say.

"We *do*," Sunny says, "but he doesn't have a particularly good idea of what it takes to see this mission through, does he? And in fact, he may actively work against our success. So, yeah!"

With a slap on the leader's rump, all three horses surge forward, and I nearly fall off my mount before I fall on the horse's mane and clutch it with the ferocity of a drowning cat, bumping wildly along, fearful that at any moment I will fall to my death. The town whirs past, and out of the corner of my eye, I see Sunny looking at me, smiling his foolish smile as we go..

Chapter 5

We eventually slow after losing our pursuers around the backs of the houses and shops of Kern.

"And where to now?" Sunny asks me.

I take a deep breath. If I knew how to ride a horse, I could try to lose him, but I don't. "That way," I say, pointing, and soon we trot in that direction.

After several minutes, we find Kat and Aden doing their best to load packs onto Mr. Wilson's plow horse in a clearing.

"Ayda!" Kat cries, running to embrace me. It hits me too - I'm alive, for the moment, and free. "Wait, who's this?" Kat asks, pointing behind me.

"The Wilder," I say, "Sunny."

"Oh," Kat says, smiling. "I'm Kat." Sunny bows in greeting.

I don't mention that Sunny wants me to sacrifice myself. Even still, I turn back to him now and say, "Thank you for your help getting away from the guards, *but* - we can manage from here. I have my own plans, and if you wouldn't mind, I'd rather go on alone."

"Yes," Sunny says. "I'm sure you do have your own plans. But it's my job to guide you. If it's any help, I think you will make it a good way towards where you think you want to go. In the meantime, why don't you allow me to help? For instance, we can return your neighbor's plow horse. After all, why take a man's livelihood when we have horses for the three of us and a pack horse?"

"Hold on," Aden says when Sunny motions to him. "I just came to help Ayda get on her way. I have school to finish."

"Every Centenary sacrifice has at least one companion for the journey," Sunny says. "But you know that, don't you?"

"Well. What about her?" Aden asks, pointing to Kat.

Sunny shakes his head. "That suggestion isn't particularly worthy of you, is it? Dear Kat isn't meant for this quest. She doesn't really have the constitution for it. She will stay here. But you – you are another matter entirely. It is your charge to go. Or am I mistaken?"

"I..." Aden's face reddens. "Alright!" he says. "I'll go."

"Good," Sunny says.

"Uh.....*No*..." I say, correcting Sunny. Neither of you is coming. Kat can come if she likes. But the two of you," I say, "are not invited."

"Actually, I am invited already," Sunny says. "It is the year of the Centenary. It is the year of the Wilder."

Kat looks on in something like amazement.

"So you're really a Wilder?" Aden asks. "My Da says you Wilders go everywhere in Landria and all over. Have you been to the Great Peak?"

"I have," Sunny says.

"Have you been to Witch Marsh?" Aden continues.

"I have," Sunny replies.

"Have you sailed on a ship?" Aden asks.

"Yes."

"Well," Aden says, "at least it's better to have a guide."

"Not," I reply as anger rises in my throat, "if our guide tries to guide me someplace I do *not* wish to *go*."

"On my oath," Sunny says, "I will not guide you where you do not wish to go. You should know, however, that as the Centenary, it will be very difficult to avoid the Pit. In fact, you will certainly meet your destiny on the road you take to avoid it."

"I will, will I?" I ask. "Well, I'm going to Witch Marsh. That's right. That's where I'm going."

Kat and Aden seem rather aghast at my announcement, but Sunny only nods with severity. "Very well," he says.

I nod and grimace. I'm still wondering if I should try to lose the Wilder when Kat asks, "What should we do with the plow horse?"

"Just let him go," Sunny replies. "He knows his way home."

Sunny steps over, gingerly unties the packs – which fall to the ground – and slaps Mr. Wilson's horse on the rump. Soon it disappears in the direction of the town.

"And now we need to be on our way," Sunny says.

"Yes," I say. "If we keep a steady pace, I think we can make it to Hook Swallow in a few days. We'll charter our passage from there."

"A solid plan," Sunny says. "Now, let's make haste before the High Minister's guards catch up with us. Like I said before, they don't understand how all of this works."

"Oh. And what don't they understand?" Kat asks.

"That Ayda must sacrifice herself willingly in Notso's pit," Sunny replies.

"I'm not sacrificing myself!" I exclaim. "And if either of you wants to go back, you can. *I'm* the one they want to kill."

Aden grimaces but doesn't move to take my offer. They both stubbornly stay by my side.

Which just leaves tall, pretty, awkward Kat who has been my best friend for as long as I can remember. And yet, I feel as though we have grown apart this last year, maybe because I never shared my secret with her. Maybe because she fits in better than I do. No one thinks she's a witch. They expect her to be a tavern server like her Ma. And if she stays here, that's all she'll ever be. But maybe that's enough for her.

"I'll miss you," Kat says as tears slide down her face. "I don't want to be a witch, Ayda. And I don't want you to be one either. And I wish you could stay too. I'm sorry…"

"At least I'll be accepted there," I say.

"I hope so," Kat says, rubbing the tears out of her eyes. She hugs me close and then races off back in the direction of town. Sunny and Aden, meanwhile, tie the packs to the other horse before Aden gets up on his own mount.

As soon as we've got the horse packed, we hear the sound of riders and shouts in the distance.

"What if they catch us?" Aden asks.

"Then they might complicate our quest," Sunny says as he mounts. "You'll have to ride sidesaddle again, Ayda."

"If they catch us," I say as I pull myself up on my horse again, "They'll give *you* back to your father," I say to Aden, "they'll send me on my way to be sacrificed, and him," I say, pointing to Sunny, "I'm not sure."

"Yes, they might," Aden says as we start off at a good little trot. "Or they might consider me a traitor." He grabs a sword at his side that I hadn't realized had been under his coat this whole time.

"Let's hope you never have to use that," Sunny says. "Taking a life is a terrible thing. Don't kill anyone if you can help it."

"Oh, that's rich," I say. "How can you say taking a life is a terrible thing when you want to take *my* life!"

"Taking a life *is* a terrible thing," Sunny says. "Giving a life, on the other hand, is a beautiful thing."

"Oh yeah, then why don't you give yours?" I ask

Sunny smiles. "For now, the lot has fallen to you, Ayda. But I have thought about it a great deal. I am willing to make that sacrifice if and when it is right to do so."

I frown sourly at this. I'm about to throw some other caustic remarks Sunny's way when we hear dogs barking nearby. My heart quickens. They have undoubtedly caught our scent.

"What do we do when the dogs catch us?" Aden asks.

Sunny smiles at him. "Dogs are friendly when you are friendly to them." He produces two pieces of jerky from his pouch.

"I guess you have everything figured out then!" I say harshly. "And what if their guards catch up with us?"

"I might have a plan," Sunny says, "but I imagine you have a plan too, or is that little book you have hidden in your vest not what I think it is?"

At this, I falter.

"What is it?" Aden asks.

I don't say anything.

"I believe," Sunny says, "that it's a book of spells."

Even greater horror washes over Aden's face than was present there when I announced destination.

"They were right about you," Aden says. "You *are* a witch!"

"So go back and leave me be, why don't you!" I yell, but Aden doesn't change his direction.

Sunny, unfazed by our bickering, asks, "So tell me, which spell do you have planned? Cursing our pursuers with blindness? Or with stabbing pains? Or a spell to give yourself strength? You should know something about the spells from that book - and maybe you have already suspected it - they are never a good idea. In fact, you should throw the book away as soon as possible."

"Wait, what do you know about magic?" Aden asks.

"More than Ayda," Sunny replies. "Everyone I have ever known who practiced witchcraft has been harmed by it, and it wouldn't surprise me if Ayda has already suffered."

"Wait - how many witches have you known?" Aden asks.

"None, I'm sure!" I say. "Look at him. He's barely older than we are. Besides, can *he* protect us? The constables have almost caught us, and you're both quibbling over a couple of spells when my life is at stake!"

"Giving your life," Sunny replies, "is not nearly so bad as what you suffer by using that book. I hope you'll understand that soon. As for what *I* might do - I *have* been known to use a little magic of my own..."

Sunny starts whispering under his breath. For a few moments, I wonder if the strange wilder boy has finally reached the end of his crazy mind until I feel a strange shift in the air. Suddenly, the world goes hazy, and I realize that a fog has lifted into our path through the woods. I have read my little spell book cover to cover, and there are no spells for fog.

"How did you do that?" I ask.

"I merely asked the water of the air to come hide us," Sunny says. But just then, the dogs, whose barking has grown louder this entire time, finally reach us.

"Ah!" Aden cries as one of the hounds nips at my horse.

But the dogs don't go for Aden or Sunny. One launches at me where I'm sitting side saddle, and I fall backwards, rolling on the ground and just missing the hooves of Sunny's horse and a tree that would have broken my neck.

I next open my eyes to find Sunny over me and a dog who whines now before gobbling down the jerky in Sunny's hand. I stand. Sunny catches the dog by the collar next, pushes its nose down, pulls the hound in close, and in another moment rises up again with his hands free.

"Aden, your sword," Sunny says, reaching out his hand.

Aden hands the scabbard over to Sunny. I reach out to stop him from killing the dog when he reaches for me instead, takes my skirt, impales it, and slashes downward. "Now turn around," he says. I'm so bewildered that I can barely say anything as he turns me around, plunges the sword into the back of my skirt, and does the same thing.

"Now we'll need to keep going," Sunny says.

I feel outraged – exposed (though I have plenty in the way of under-britches). But I don't have any time to declare my anger. The sound of horses nearing us hurries me up onto my own mount. Sunny quickly adjusts the stirrups to my feet, and we're soon racing through the woods behind our Wilder leader, who must be able to see through the fog better than I can.

My heart beats wildly as we ride and I feel untethered inside, like my whole life spins wildly like a top, spinning and spinning, waiting to crash and fall.

Chapter 6

By the time my heartbeat finally slows we have escaped our pursuers. The fog did its work and we simply rode and rode until eventually they weren't back there anymore.

And now we continue to ride, and as the day begins to wane, Sunny finally calls for us to stop. Once the basics of our camp are set, I volunteer to bake the bread while Aden and Sunny go to the stream to fish. I get water, mix it in the flour, add a pinch of salt, and start my fire. Then I do what I actually intended to do when I sent the boys off to fish. I pull out my spell book.

Compared to the books in the schoolhouse, my spell book is poorly made - just a couple of thin boards and leaves of paper tied together with string. Its words are written in a rough hand, and some of the letters are difficult to read. The witch symbols, however, were drawn with care - enough care for me to replicate them.

The book came to me one night when a passing traveler handed it to me in the tavern – just walked over and handed it to me and didn't say a word before walking straight out to the road, never to be seen in Kern again.

When I cracked open the cover, I almost dropped the book in surprise when I saw the symbols because we're taught against such things in the schoolhouse. And I could have gotten rid of it right then - thrown it in the waste, pushed it into the fire, but instead I hid it in my pocket. I was there helping Kat that night, but I didn't breathe a word about it to her. Instead, I took it home into my little partitioned room and hid it in my drawer.

Nearly a month later, huddled behind a loose board with a candle, I took the spell book from my drawer and barely dared to breathe as I read the book's words for the first time. I studied all the symbols that corresponded to the words of power and read the instructions on how to say them. From these words, many different spells in this other language were formed. But the book made it clear that saying the spells was not enough. For them to actually work, the book dictated that the symbols had to be grounded somehow to the caster's body, whether by carving them into the skin and flesh, burning or branding them in, or, as most witches chose, tattooing.

I, of course, didn't know anything about tattooing until I got suspended for kicking Roland in his crotch and spent the next two days helping out at Mrs. Cartwright's salon. Apart from piercing girls' ears and styling hair, Mrs. Cartwright happened to learn tattooing during her training at the beauty school in Milna, and so, for my two days sweeping up hair and doing whatever else she asked, Mrs. Cartwright gave me a tattoo of a small tree on my ankle and answered all the questions I peppered her with as she went. I already had a set of bone needles for sewing, and, with all the natural materials we collected for my mother's herbal remedies, it wasn't hard for me to make my own inks. After that, it was just the process of getting them on my body, and the understanding that I would have to hide them or face dire consequences. I only finished my tattooing a few nights ago.

I cook the flatbread while I consider what spells will best help me on my journey, and I quickly hide the book away again when Sunny and Aden return with a line of fish. With the help of a knife Aden produces from our packs, I help clean the trout. Aden gushes about the experience of catching the fish (which you should try, he says to me).

We eat silently around the fire, clean up, and then make our beds around the embers that have not yet gone out.

The sun disappears beyond the horizon, and the night looms large above us with twinkling stars and a luminous moon.

As I look up at the night sky, I think over my plan to ditch the boys in the morning. I'll get up before them and leave them behind. I don't feel bad about it. Sunny says he won't make me do anything I don't want to do, but I can already tell he wants to needle me towards sacrificing myself, so why subject myself to that? And Aden will be better off back home. They say he's to become a minister. A journey with me will ruin his prospects for that if he doesn't go back soon and make up a story to their liking.

"Ayda," Aden whispers quietly.

"*What?*" I ask, realizing my voice is a bit harsher than I mean.

"Nothing," he says. "I mean. I guess I want to say...sorry."

"For what?" I ask.

"I should have stuck up for you," he says. "And I didn't."

"I don't need anyone to stick up for me," I reply. "I've done just fine by myself this far. And I'm going to a place where that's the law of the land. I'll be fine. You're the one I'm worried about. You should go back before you get yourself hurt."

"Well, like I said," Aden continues, "I'm sorry. I was going to be a minister, but I feel like I've already failed."

"What are you talking about?" I ask. "You'll fit right in. Did you know they rigged the lottery for me to be chosen? That's all you cassocks want, to get rid of undesirables. And don't even bother to deny it."

Aden doesn't reply.

Then something strange happens. From the light of the last ember of our fire, I think I see the gleam of a tear in Aden's eye. But that can't be right. He turns his head.

And that's it. We don't speak anymore after that. Then, at some point I don't remember, I fall asleep.

Chapter 7

When I wake up sore on the hard earth in the early morning hours, I decide to make good on my plan of escape. Silently, I rise and tiptoe over to the horses. I saddle the one I think was mine from yesterday (it's hard to tell in the dark). I put the packs on the pack horse with a certain amount of exertion, and try to hush the horses from whinnying and stomping around too loudly as I finish. I follow Sunny's example and nimbly tie the pack horse's lead to mine before mounting up - torn skirt and all. Then I urge my two horses to walk quietly out of our little camp.

I sigh in relief after a few minutes of walking and try to settle into the journey, but my anxieties still linger. *Could Sunny and Aden still catch me?* Not if my lead is large enough. *Can horses injure themselves in the dark?* Fortunately, there's a good-sized moon out tonight, and I decide we'll only walk - at least until daylight. There are many other things, of course, that can go wrong in my plan, many diversions and dead ends I might encounter, not the least of which is running into the pursuers the Ministry has sent after me.

Danger hides in every shadow - or at least that's how I feel. Maybe it's better that I am on my own, but the safety I felt in our little group, whether real or imagined, is now gone, and I almost regret my decision to leave. There's nothing for it now, though.

I keep riding and riding, and the sky eventually brightens overhead before the sun shows itself through the trees and paints beautiful colors in the sky. This beauty and illumination give me the confidence to urge my horse into a trot. And renewing my determination, I retrace the steps of my plan in my mind. Eventually, I will reach the Swallow River. Now, if I were on the highway, I could take that directly to Hook Swallow, but as it is, I must try to skirt around the settlements and follow the river all the way to the sea, where I will find the port and ships, including ones from Witch Marsh that trade spices and other food commodities with Zandria.

If I can get on one of those ships, even as some sort of lowly worker scrubbing decks, I will have my passage to Witch Marsh and my goal.

I'm thinking about these things when I reign in and stop on a little ridge. I look out from this high point to try to map my path forward over the land. I even look for signs of the river in the distance, but all my distant searching ends when I hear a sound somewhere below. I glance down and realize the highway runs along the bottom of the ridge, and there on the highway are a couple of riders with swords on their belts, spears at their sides, and the emblem of the Zandrian Guard on their chests.

My heart quickens. Maybe they don't see me. Then one of them points up at me. The other shouts, and now they're galloping in my direction. All the while I sit here, frozen in my saddle. Fortunately, they're slowed down by the slope of the ridge. Nevertheless, they urge their horses to go up it, shouting at me to come down and give myself up.

I panic. I don't trust my riding skills enough to outride them. That leaves only one other option for my escape...

Shakily, I dismount. I drop my little spell book, trying to get it out of my vest, and just barely catch it before it goes sliding down the hill.

"Hey girl, put your hands where we can see them!"

My fingers feel numb as I flip the book open to the one spell I think might work in this situation. I clear my throat, which suddenly feels dry and desolate. I try to read as clearly as I can with the two guardsmen at the forefront of my mind, but the words feel like tar in my mouth. *"Tlahan ay mya sahlu dai narakah, yab yarha ayan nala sa!"*

Even as the last syllable leaves my lips, I'm certain I've messed it up, and I begin to tremble as the riders near me. But then a searing pain rips straight through my self-pitying thoughts. I clutch my abdomen and fall to my knees, trying desperately not to throw up. I struggle to breathe, and when I try to push myself back up from the ground, I can't see my hands. Everything's gone.

I feel lightheaded. I can't focus. *Breathe in, breathe out,* I tell myself. *Breathe in, breathe out. Breathe in, breathe out.*

When I've steadied myself – when I can finally think straight – I grasp at my eyes, which are thankfully still behind my eyelids. That's a relief, but not much when I have to conclude that my spell has backfired on me.

I'm a witch - there's no denying that now. Unfortunately, I'm also a terrible witch.

Unwelcome tears well up in my eyes and stream down my face. My shame quickly turns to anger, though. I clench my fists and hit the ground as I wait dismally for the guardsmen to come and take me into custody, wondering what they will do if I lash out and try to fight them. When I finally stop to listen for their coming, though, I am only able to hear the sounds of their distress in the distance. Their horses neigh wildly, but I can't tell exactly what's happening. The shouts continue, but then, eventually, they fade in the distance. As the minutes pass, I come to the strange conclusion that I am alone and that the spell must have affected them as it did me.

The comforting nuzzle of my horse's nose on my face reminds me that not all is lost, and I grab hold of his neck to pull myself to my feet.

The movement, though, reawakens my awareness of the burning feeling in my abdomen. Strangely, the pain feels mildly familiar, and as my fingers feel down to my stomach, I realize that my pain is in the exact place where I tattooed one of the witch symbols. In fact, it feels like the tattoo is freshly pierced into my skin.

Hugging my horse, I try to consider what options are available to me. I doubt the guardsmen I encountered will soon be able to come after me, but the chance that more might be riding nearby or that someone else might come along the road still terrifies me. Even still, I know I can't stay standing here forever. I'm basically helpless, though.

There's only one thing I can think of to do. It's not even a very good idea. In fact, it's almost worse than doing nothing. Reluctantly, though, I raise my voice and hope the right people hear.

"Sunny! Aden!" I cry, trying to remember what direction I came from. I lean my head that way and continue. "Sunny! Aden! Help!"

"Ayda!" I hear from far off. It sounds like Aden. I take a deep breath and call out again. He replies again. We continue exchanging calls until I can hear hooves coming up the ridge.

I'm relieved, but I also feel conflicted about being rescued. Worse, I'm once again stuck in Aden and Sunny's company.

"We found you," Aden says as he dismounts his horse. "Sunny said we would, but I have to admit, I didn't believe him. I thought you were done with us. Hey, what are you looking at?"

"Nothing," I say, suddenly embarrassed. "I've blinded myself. I can't see anything. I came upon some guardsmen. They're gone, but...I..."

"You left us," Sunny says, "but here we are again, ready to help you find your way."

"Yes," I reply, taking a deep breath. "Thank you." I pause, "Is there anything that can be done about my eyes?"

"Of course," Sunny says. "The main thing, though, is to realize that your eyes aren't any different than they were before. Your spell told them that they can't see, and they believe it. Compared to the other lies you believe, this one should be easy to correct."

"*Oh?*" I ask, suddenly feeling defensive again. "*Really?* And what *other* lies do I believe?"

"Quite a few," Sunny says. "But the most pressing one right now is that you believe that no one else loves you or cares about you, which is why you don't think you can trust anyone to help you."

"Oh yeah?" I say. "Is that so? And I suppose you want to tell me that you care about me? Even though you want me to go and sacrifice myself in the Pit?"

"Just because something's hard to believe, doesn't mean it isn't true," Sunny says. "Now, would you like me to help you with your eyes?"

I don't answer right away. "*Yes,*" I say, biting the word like a sour apple.

"Your stomach hurts here? Can I see the sore?" He asks.

I lift my shirt. The cool touch of Sunny's fingers brushes over my blistering sore. Then, as soon as his fingers leave, the pain goes with it. My shirt drops back down, and I am left in wonderment. I grew up in the house of a healer, so I know for certain that no salve or brew can do what his fingers just did.

"I still can't see," I say.

"About that," Sunny says. "Do you know what you said when you cast your spell?"

"No," I shake my head.

"Haven't you ever thought how foolish it might be to say words you don't actually understand?"

"Uh..." I say, shaking my head. "...I guess?"

"Oh, right!" Aden says, butting in. "What if you said something really embarrassing?"

"Wait - did I say something embarrassing?" I ask.

"The words of your spell," Sunny says, "were these: 'I blind my soul in darkness, but *your* eyes will not see.' And the symbol on your stomach is the word 'blind.' Now do you understand?" Sunny asks.

"Uh...no," I reply.

"The quickest way to regain your sight," Sunny says, "is to not be blind anymore - but not the blindness here." Sunny puts my hand up over my eyes. "But here," he says, putting my hand on my chest.

"And what am I supposed to see with - what would you call them? - these *inner* eyes?"

"Everything," Sunny replies. "But let's start with something you can grasp right now. This is what I want you to see - your mother didn't mean to hurt you by keeping you in Kern all these years."

I feel anger burn through me even as he says it. "*Then why did she do it?*" I ask acidly.

Then Aden, not Sunny, replies, "Because she thought she was doing what was best for you."

"Oh, yeah," I say, "and what would *you* know about it?"

"More than you'd think," Aden says.

"Really?" I say. "You're a cassock. What do you know about being an outcast? What do you know about being looked down on? What do you know about being hated? – Hated so much that someone tries to get you sacrificed?"

"She can't see," Sunny says. "It is beyond her why you've come along on this journey. She's blinded, Aden. Even with the gift of the Centenary – true sight – there is still much she will be blind to if she doesn't open her eyes."

"I know why Aden's here - *you* made him come along," I say accusingly.

"No," Sunny says. "I reminded him of his charge. But it was a charge that I did not give him."

"Oh, then who gave it to him?" I ask.

I listen to the silence, but no answer comes quickly to fill it, and finally Sunny says, "It is one thing to know something, and another thing to *know* it. I can tell you the end. It's quite simple - you are loved. You don't know this, though. Your anger and pain blind you to it. Even now, Aden won't be able to open your eyes, but it might just be the start you need, and it might help you with your eyes. Aden, tell her, who gave you the charge?"

"My...*mother*..." Aden says.

"But...wait...you don't have a mother," I say, recalling that she died when he was born.

"*Our* mother," Aden says again.

Even though my grip on my horse's bridle remains firm, I suddenly feel unsteady, like I'm about to fall over, or the ground might move from beneath my feet. "*Our* mother?" I ask.

"And father," Aden says, "Da."

I swallow. Somehow I've let go of the bridle, and I feel myself going. Before I quite know it, I'm rolling down the ridge in the darkness of my unseeing eyes. And I have no idea where I'll stop.

Chapter 8

I do stop. And moan. And moan some more. But even though I feel bruised and broken, my mind begins to whirl with activity.

Everyone in Kern has heard the story, after all, and whispered it back and forth for years and years now. Mr. Jeffries' wife fell ill. That's how it all started. Then, together, he and his wife traveled throughout Zandria in search of a healer for her ailments, but Mr. Jefferies didn't return for two whole years. And when he did, he came home with a baby boy and without his wife. He explained that Mrs. Jeffries had indeed been healed. She became pregnant, gave birth to a baby boy, and then tragically died in childbirth.

Ma, on the other hand, would never tell me much about how we came to live in Kern - so far away from our kinfolk in Fishton. She would say things like she just wanted a different view of the world, to see something different. She journeyed and journeyed until she happened to stop in Kern and thought, 'Wow, what a great place to stay!'

I always found that last part hard to swallow. Why, after all, would she stay in Kern? There's very little for us there except disdain and discrimination. But now, all the pieces are coming together in my mind. She must have come to Kern mere months after Mr. Jeffries returned with his newborn son, and with her own babe in tow – me. That's the timeline.

Ma is a healer. Of course, she met the Jeffries when they searched for a cure. What else happened after they met? And Mr. Jeffries's back pain became a convenient cover for meeting my mother week after week.

But why had Mr. Jeffries taken Aden and not me? I can almost see him sitting across from me and reasoning quite convincingly that he thought a son of his would do well in his world and might even join the Ministry - quite like Aden seems promised to do. And that I would do well in Ma's world of healing - except that I haven't. No, things have gone quite a different way for me.

"Ayda," Aden says when he reaches me. I look up and see his face with my eyes.

"So you've been my brother this whole time, and it never occurred to you to get Roland to leave Kat and me alone," I say, pushing his help away as I struggle to get up and dust myself off.

"Good," Sunny says as he joins us at the bottom of the ridge. "You're seeing again. New understandings always help to shake the blindness off. And yet, I don't think you understand yet, do you?"

"Would you just stop it?" I ask. "I've had enough of you. Enough of both of you!"

"Ayda, wait!" Aden calls as I go marching back up the ridge to my horse and packhorse. I don't listen to him, though. I don't care if he *is* my brother. Why didn't I figure this out sooner? We almost even have the same name! - Ayda, Aden?

When I reach the summit, I pick up my little spell book and dust it off.

"I didn't know!" Aden cries as he runs up after me. "They didn't tell me!"

I don't want to hear it.

Aden just reaches me, then we both look across to the highway and find several more Zandorian Guards gathered there before they notice us. One gives a shout, and Aden and I turn to each other and think the same thing. In another moment, we mount our horses and are racing off down the ridge again.

Sunny catches up to us, and soon we're riding through the woods and glancing over our shoulders at the guards as they try to catch up to us.

"Don't worry," Sunny says. "It's not time yet for them to catch you."

"Whether it's time or not," I say, "they're pretty close to doing it."

"It's time, I think," Sunny says, "for another lesson on sacrifice. Do you see those hills in the distance?"

Aden and I both nod.

"There you will find the town of Riverbend. Hire a barge to take you down the river to Hookswallow. I will meet up with you there."

With that, Sunny reins in his horse and slows down. I look over my shoulder and watch as several of the guardsmen who were nearest to catching us are caught up by his surrender. One pulls him off his horse and dismounts. I just see him strike Sunny across the back of his head, dropping him to the ground, when the trees finally block my view of him.

We are not safe yet, though. Other guardsmen still pursue us.

I hold on tightly, untrained as I am in riding, and Aden directs us around obstacles as we gallop through the woods.

"I'll stall them," Aden says. "You go on. If they catch me, they won't kill me."

He didn't see, though, what they did to Sunny. Before he can slow his horse down, I pull out my little spell book and call out the same words I had spoken before. This time, however, even as I make the sounds of those foreign words, I comprehend them. *"I blind my soul in darkness, but your eyes will not see!"* I clutch my stomach in pain but force myself to look back as the guards bring their hands to their faces and slow their horses to a halt. Have I hurt them? But then, in the next moment, my own eyes dim.

Wow, I'm really bad at this.

As I look about myself, I realize that my blindness isn't quite as bad as last time. I can make out the world around me in shades of gray and nearly indistinct lines. I can tell almost immediately, however, that I am still functionally blind.

"Ayda - did you just do *more* witchcraft?" Aden asks, incensed.

"*Yes!*" I reply. "Now tell me - are we safe?"

"Wait, are you blind again, too?" he asks.

I grit my teeth and try not to growl. "*I am.*" I give a huff, but I doubt he can hear it over the galloping. "*You're welcome!*" I shout.

We don't talk after that.

A few more minutes of rough riding pass by before we bring the horses to a trot. After a little longer, Aden tells me we have arrived, but the abstract shapes of buildings don't tell me much about what the town looks like. I hear conversations in the distance, the movement of people and animals, but that's all.

I know from geography lessons in school that Riverbend is a sizable inland city and the largest one nearest to Kern. If anyone in Kern has been anywhere, it's to Riverbend to the east or Milna to the west. I, of course, have never been anywhere. But I did study Riverbend in detail at one time because I deluded myself into thinking it was far enough away. I would escape here to live without the stigma of my mother's work hanging over me. Eventually, though, I realized people from Kern would find me there and ignite the same ridicule and hatred in my new home, which is how I eventually settled on going further to the logging camp in Bayton and then later to go even further to Witch Marsh.

"This way," Aden says, leading the horses and me somewhere else. He tells me to stay with the horses, which he hardly needs to say, because - where else can a blind girl go? Then he comes back and informs me, "We're going to sell the horses to the owner of the barge. It will cover our trip, and we'll make a tidy profit that will hopefully get us where we're going. Also, a woman over there saw the condition of your skirt."

I immediately feel my entire face turn to flame.

"She asked if I wanted to buy a skirt from her," Aden continues, "but I told her I would buy riding britches or nothing at all."

My face still feels like it's on fire. "How am I going to get them on?" I ask.

"There's an outhouse over there," Aden says. "Do you want me to, uh...come in with you?"

"No!" I shout before realizing I shouldn't be making a scene.

I get into my new pants in the outhouse. I don't want to think about what difficulty I overcame in that little, smelly building.

After this, Aden leads me by hand to board the barge. The only thing I can think, though, is that walking around in pants feels strange, and I'm glad that I can hold on to him while I get used to it.

"Come on," Aden says, leading me further on. "There are some seats up at the front of the barge."

When I sit down, the seat is hard, wooden, but at least it has a back - and that's all I can tell about it. I think I'm in the farthest one, and Aden is beside me. I can feel the rocking of the water beneath me and hear its gentle lapping on the side of the barge.

"We're casting off now," Aden says.

"Are we?" I ask, barely able to make out the shore when I strain to see it through my restrained vision. And there, strangely, I think I see something looking back at me. What a peculiar thought. Did I really see that? Were those eyes? It's strange enough to see eyes in my blindness, but they don't look like any kind I've ever seen before. In fact, they look more like darker shades of black, like voids somehow trying to suck me in from across the way.

"Hey," I say to Aden. "What's that?"

"What's what?" he asks.

"That...the...*is there anything over there?*"

"A bird just flew off," Aden says. "A raven, I think."

And just like that, the eyes of darkness are gone.

Chapter 9

After what seems like forever, we finally get started down the river, which at least means the Zandorian Guards won't catch us for the moment, but those dark eyes won't leave the canvas of my mind. It's like they're painted there permanently. Did I imagine them? Am I just too jumpy? Too anxious. I look and look and look, but eventually I give up. Trying to make out different shades of darkness is just too hard. Strangely, though, when I turn towards Aden, I have a distinct feeling that the darkness around him is brighter...? Is that weird?

"So what do you think about Sunny?" Aden asks eventually.

"About *Sunny?*" I say. "He's weird."

"I mean, what kind of weird?" Aden asks.

"Not as weird as me being your sister," I say. "Now *that's* weird. I get it. Our parents found each other in West Zandria. They liked each other. I get it that your father didn't want to marry Ma because any association with someone on the wrong side of the Ministry would be - what? - too costly for him? Would his position in the church be taken? Would he get excommunicated?"

"I don't know," Aden says. "I don't know why."

"You don't?" I say. "Well, I guess I never will then because I'm never going back. He had his chance to be in my life."

"He came to save you," Aden replies in anguish. "I'm sure of it! But he got hurt - he fell off the horse! And he told me to catch up with you and keep you safe. And I didn't know what he meant then, but you were chosen, and then I saw Ma at the Tavern when I tried to follow after you."

"I don't *care*," I say. "I *don't care!* If he asks after all this, I'm grateful. But if he wants to see me, he can come to me where I'm going." I remembered just in time not to say Witch Marsh aloud on this barge. "And Sunny can come see me there too, because I don't want to have anything to do with him, either."

"Well, uh…" Aden says. "What I was going to say is that I think Sunny's a wizard."

"Really?" I ask. "And where'd you get that idea – one of your books?"

"*No*," Aden says defensively. "He has magic. And it's good magic – nature magic. Not like the magic from…you know where."

"Ugh!" I exclaim. "Of course you would think that!"

"Some people," Aden says, "say there were people who practiced nature magic out in the West Zandria. Maybe it was a long time ago. Maybe they're all gone, but I think that's what Da was looking for when he traveled out that way and found our Ma."

That catches me by surprise, but I dismiss it. "I'm pretty sure Ma doesn't have any sort of magic if that's what you're thinking," I say. "I've lived with her all my life, and I've never seen her raise the mist or anything else like what we saw Sunny do."

"Well," Aden says, "I don't know. But if it can be taught, maybe Sunny can teach you to be a wizard. Isn't that what you want? Power?"

"Not just power," I say, shaking my head. "I want…I want…" I start, but I can't finish it. How can I explain that the people of Witch Marsh are my people, that I'll finally be understood and accepted, that I'll finally belong?

"It's not *that*," I say finally.

We don't speak much after that. I get bored, but I don't want to talk with Aden anymore, so instead I listen to the water as it laps the side of the barge and wonder whether the water is blue or some shade of green. I wonder whether Aden brought a book to read. He always had one back at school tucked under his desk. I wonder what his room looks like at his father's estate house. I wonder why he's who he is, and I'm who I am.

And in this quiet darkness, I realize that I haven't thought much about being sacrificed in the Pit for a while, so I think about that. What will happen if I'm not sacrificed? Or if no one is sacrificed? Does it have to be me? I imagine Sunny knows the answers to my questions, but I hope I never get the chance to ask him.

After a while, I decide to ignore my thoughts and rest my head against my shoulder. I relax. I barely feel myself drifting off to sleep.

"Hey," a voice says. "Wake up."

"Aden?"

"Of course."

"What is it?" I ask, sitting up.

"The bargeman says we're nearing Hook Swallow. You missed the mid-day meal. Here - have some bread."

As I stuff the roll into my mouth, Aden leans forward and says in a low whisper, "We'll have to be careful. Some of the Guard may be looking for us at the docks – or maybe the barge will be raided by witch pirates."

"*Witch pirates?*" I ask, realizing too late that I've spoken too loudly.

"*Shhh!*" Aden says, then a moment later, under his voice again. "What? You haven't heard of them? Da gets all the official memorandums and warnings. Witch pirates are Witchlanders who raid the coastal towns now and then. They don't raid as much as they did before the war. I expect they're afraid of Ministry forces."

"I've never heard of them," I say, softly this time, but secretly I'm thinking of how getting to Witch Marsh might be even easier than I thought.

"Your eyes look red. Did you sleep?" I ask.

"Not much - wait," he says. "You can see my eyes?"

I gasp. "Yeah, I guess I can."

I look around, and I look everywhere. At the crates and barrels, at the trees and farmsteads that pass by on the shore, to the bargeman who works his pole with a steady rhythm and who glares at me, to the bright, warming sun.

After a day of blindness, even the murky waters mesmerize me. "I wish I could take a swim," I say as I look longingly down into the waters.

"You can swim?" Aden asks as he turns around to look with me.

"Sure, I can," I say. "What? You never learned to swim, *cassock boy?*"

"Well, I read about it," Aden says. "I know all the strokes – there's backstroke and forestroke and goosestroke. I've seen diagrams. I've even read about the swimming races in the North Bay."

"You read too much," I say, and with that I grab his shoulders and give him a big shove over the railing, but I catch him by the waist right with his head an arm-span from the water and let him hang there wailing piteously for a few moments before I pull him back up into his seat.

Aden breathes raggedly and I see tears forming at the edge of his eyes, threatening to break out into a full-fledged weeping.

"Hey – I, I'm sorry," I say while Aden catches his breath. "I...I just – you'll never learn to swim unless you get in. I mean, it's too cold right now. I...I'm sorry."

Aden doesn't reply, and I sit there for a few minutes feeling rather poorly about myself. Maybe I really should be alone in the world. I just have to get to Witch Marsh. Then everything will be the way it should be. But until then, how will I make things up to Aden?

"Hey," I say, "Uh...what are those birds flying above us?" I ask, realizing just how feeble my attempt at patching things up really is.

"They're swallows," Aden says, wiping the tears from the edges of his eyes with his sleeve. "You know - they're *Hook* Swallows."

"Really?" I ask. "I always thought the name was about fishing."

"No – *you didn't!*" Aden cries, laughing now, and I breath a small sigh of relief.

"Well, not everyone knows everything about *everything*," I say a little defensively.

"Of course, of course," Aden concedes. "No. Hook Swallows migrate north in the spring and build nests of mud under the bridges and rock faces all throughout this area. Look - do you see those mud-looking things under the eaves of that farmhouse?"

"Oh...right, I do," I say. I see a single bird wing up to one of the little mud mounds and disappear into it before another bird emerges from a different mound and wings away.

"They hatch their chicks in there, and the parents come back to feed them," Aden says.

"Wow," I say, "an even smaller living space than our hut back home." I wonder what it would be like to live in such a mound and be fed by birds swooshing in. Eventually, though, the chicks must leave the mud nest behind and fly away.

After a while longer, the bargeman finally calls, "Docks ahead." He points.

Before I know it, the bargeman's boy is securing the mooring. We've arrived. All the buildings beyond the docks must be in the city of Hook Swallow.

We're about to exit the barge when I notice a canoe coming around from the other side of a fishing vessel - a canoe paddled by a young man with puffy hair pushed somewhat unsuccessfully under a wide-brimmed hat. Instantly, I know that my goofy-looking guide has returned.

"Want a ride?" Sunny asks with a smile as he pulls up on the other side of the barge.

"Sunny!" Aden cries in excitement. "I thought –"

"–That I couldn't escape the guards and meet you in Hookswallow as I said?" Sunny asks. "Well, don't worry about it. You don't know me that well yet, Aden, but one thing you'll soon understand is that I always keep my word. Now, we had better move on before the guard searches the vessel. I'm sure riders have already arrived with your description."

Even as Sunny speaks I find the guardsman on the dock. He's talking to someone, seemingly distracted from noticing us at the moment. But how long will that last, I wonder?

"How did you get here?" Aden asks as he climbs into Sunny's canoe. Warily, I follow.

"Oh, I have my ways," Sunny replies as he begins paddling.

"How enigmatic," Aden says.

"Or suspicious," I counter.

"If you must know, I rode a series of stags."

"Like...male deer?" I ask.

"Yes," Sunny says with a straight face.

"Do you know all the animals?" Aden asks. "Ayda had a pretty strange reaction to a raven at the beginning of our journey."

"You did?" Sunny asks. "Did it say anything to you?"

"*What?*" I ask in surprise, "No. I couldn't even see them. It was just like dark - a darker darkness. I don't know."

Sunny nods grimly.

"What was it?" Aden asks.

"A chimera," Sunny replies. "They are the creatures of the scarabs. You should avoid them if you can. But if Ayda still wants to journey to Witch Marsh, I'm afraid that will be impossible. What is your decision, Ayda? Are you still set on going to Witch Marsh? Or would you like to go the much easier route to the Pit up the Milna River?"

"I told you - *I'm not going to the Pit!*" I say angrily. "I'm going to Witch Marsh!"

"Well then, get back out of the boat," Sunny says as he pulls back up to the dock.

"What?" I ask. "What are you doing?"

Several Zandrain Guards walk down the dock in our direction now. They see the alarm in my eyes and begin to run.

"Sunny!" I cry, "Start rowing!"

Sunny sits there, dispassionate and unmoving as I try to grab the oar from him. "Not everything is as it seems, Ayda. Seeing you do not see."

Before I can make a reply, hands grab me up out of the canoe and put me onto the dock. Aden tries to draw his sword, but Sunny convinces him to re-sheath it, and in another few moments, we are all being roughly dragged through the market.

"I hope you're happy!" I shout at Sunny.

"I'm not happy," Sunny replies evenly. "Remember," Sunny says. "You chose this."

I'm about to say more when a bag is thrust over my head, and I suddenly find that I've been made blind once again.

Chapter 10

Darkness. Infuriating darkness.

A guard grips my shoulder forcefully and pushes me up the steps into some sort of carriage, leaving me to stew in my anger as we lurch forward moments later. Soon I hear sellers hocking their wares and customers haggling. This general din of activity tells me that we're driving through the market After a few more moments, though, we turn, and the sounds change again. Now I can only hear seagulls.

Finally, the guard pulls me out of the carriage and yanks the bag from over my head, revealing Aden and Sunny's faces as well.

We are at the docks again - but not the same docks, I think, because the ships I see here are much larger than our barge. No - these must be seagoing vessels.

After a few moments of waiting, a procession of Cassocks, including the red-robed Gerald Fry, appears before us.

"Ayda!" Minister Fry says, stepping forward. I strain against the guard holding me as I shrink back from the High Minister.

"It seems that you've made it all the way to the Port on your own," Fry continues. "Good job. We didn't know, of course, that you had given yourself over to witchcraft, but I have to say, it makes me feel a lot better about our choice. And, of course, if you were anyone *but* the Centenary, we would deal with you quite severely. You see, I don't care for these witchfolk.

In fact, they're an abomination, but as it turns out, we are not as free of them as I would like. On a happier note, we'll be free of you soon enough."

I don't really know what to say to that.

"And it seems you also took one of the sons of our Deacons along with you," Minister Fry continues. "Am I to suppose that he has been steeped in witchcraft as well?"

"I'm not a witch!" Aden cries.

"He's not," I say more evenly.

"Even so, now your stain is on him," Minister Fry says. "My, oh my - what to do with someone who conspires with witches. Hmm..."

No wonder Mr. Jeffries could never marry Ma openly, I think, shaking my head angrily.

"And last, but not least, is the traitorous Wilder," Minister Fry spits.

"As far as betrayal goes," Sunny says, "why don't you get on and do what you intend to do?"

Fry's smile freezes on his face and somehow morphs into the most hateful, condescending smile I've ever seen.

"You know," the High Minister says, "I see now why some of the notes from my predecessors mention doing away with your position or even going out to lay siege to your island home. I thought these suggestions were a little extreme when I first read them - after all, the Wilders are part of our story - but now - *now* I understand. Somehow you bring out something inside of me that's..." Fry laughs and clutches his hands in front of him as though he's imagining shaking Sunny vigorously.

"Oh, we Wilders have known for quite some time what sort of bargain you Zandrians struck with Witch Marsh at the end of the last war. Isn't that your tribute there?"

I look at where Sunny points and find another handful of guardsmen herding a group of children onto the dock towards a ship that I hadn't noticed earlier - one crewed by people in dark robes. My pulse quickens.

"I'll let you know that I *inherited* that agreement," Fry argues angrily. "Would you rather we were still at war? A few are sacrificed for the many. Isn't that why Ayda goes to her doom? Spare me your indignation, *Wilder!*"

"You know nothing of the centenary sacrifice," Sunny replies. "You pretend to speak for Sandor, but your mouth is full of Notso's words."

High Minister Fry has somehow become even more incensed than he was before. "Oh, I suppose you visit with Sandor regularly, do you? Enough of this. Guards - *seize the idolator!*"

Sunny steps away from the nearest guard, who tries to jump at him and easily evades him as the guard goes reeling to the wooden boards of the docks. The rest of the high minister's forces surround him now, but they are more wary as they move closer to him.

Sunny, as usual, doesn't seem concerned at all. In fact, he turns to them and asks, "Isn't this city named after all those birds circling above?" And then, as another guard tries to grab Sunny, the Wilder sidesteps and blows a shrill whistle with two fingers in his mouth. He evades another guard as well, but my attention - and that of the guards - soon turns to a strange sound rising in our ears. I can't place it - and then, just as I figure out what it is, birds are everywhere.

Hundreds of hook swallows wing past and around Sunny, leaving the guards stumbling around blindly in the thick of them, still trying to grab him, but by the time the swallows clear out into the sky, Sunny is gone.

The High Minister, now bespeckled by bird poop, marches over to them in irate fury. "*Find him!* What are you waiting for? *Go!*" He shoves one of the guardsmen and kicks another, and the rest of them and the other ministers race off in every direction.

Two darkly robed people, meanwhile, approach us while Ministry Fry tries to recompose himself and I try to study our new visitors in earnest. One of them is a woman whose luminously pale face is covered by spiderweb-thin tattoos. The designs appear to be the markings from my now confiscated spell book - some of the very same ones I copied onto my own skin. But when she pulls her hood back, I realize that she is young, not much older than me.

The other person's hood remains in place, and I can only see darkness there. But on top of this figure's shoulder rides something shaped like a monkey. It has no fur, though, and instead looks like it is made up entirely of ink or tar. But its eyes are what really grab my attention. They look like little caverns of darkness - darker than the gloop that makes up the creature. My heart quickens at the sight of them.

Minister Fry, still wiping bird droppings from his face, steps forward to address these two strangers. "Captain Dara," he says, trying to feign his regular cheerfulness, "the girl here is Ayda Cellars, and we have nominated her as our Centenary Sacrifice. I would like to extend our thanks for your help in seeing that she is sacrificed properly."

"Of course," Captain Dara says, bowing her head lightly. "But you sent a delegation concerning the Wilder, who you promised to turn over to our care in exchange for a lessening of your tribute."

"Did I? - I *did*, didn't I?" Minister Fry says with a forced laugh. "You know, he was right here a moment ago, but as you may have seen, he has slipped away. Don't worry. We should have him back soon. Any minute now."

"But you do not have him *now*," Dara says, "which means that your number of tribute is *short*."

"Captain Dara!" Minister Fry says as the young witch steps closer. "I'm sure we can come to some sort of agreement."

"Maybe we should take you instead," Dara says as the High Minister shrinks back. I realize now that we are almost entirely alone. Only one guard holds Aden and me. Everyone else has gone off in search of Sunny.

"We'll get you the rest of the tributes!" Ministry Fry shouts, but Dara grabs him by the collar. "We'll add ten percent," he cries, "No, twenty!"

"That sounds about right," Dara says, letting the High Minister go.

"And we'll start with this one here," Minister Fry says, motioning to Aden.

"The girl's companion?" Dara asks.

"Yes," Fry answers.

"Wait!" Aden cries. "I'm a deacon's son! You can't give me to witches!"

"A good deacon's son would have *escaped* by now," Fry says contemptuously. "Your fate is on your own head." He turns back to Captain Dara and says, "And I assume you'll accept this advance?"

"He'll do," she replies. "The rest you can bring to the Pit."

"The *Pit!?*" Fry squeaks.

"Yes," Dara says. "Have them ready at your miner's camp. We will send for them when we arrive. And if you *can't* manage this..." Dara smiles, "...we can just take them from wherever we see fit."

"No, no..." Fry says as sweat glistens on his forehead, "...we'll have them ready."

"You'd better," Dara says. Then she turns to me. Is she appraising me? Do I look like what she thought a centenary sacrifice would look like?

"Hello, Ayda," Dara says, with a light smile on her pale face.

"Uh...*hi*," I say.

"You'll come with us now," she says, extending a hand.

I take the captain's hand, and she leads me to her ship. The scarab (or so Sunny called it) and its chimera walk closely behind us, making me only a little uneasy.

"Welcome to the Spell Racer," Dara says. The closer I get, the more the ship stands out from those around it. It has black sails and a hull and railings covered in elaborate carvings, the master stroke of which is a figurehead at the front - a carved skeleton whose face appears to be shrieking. The rest of the carvings are bones and witch symbols, and the name *Spell Racer*. I walk up the gangplank to the main deck and try to feel like this is exactly where I want to be.

The moment is only partly ruined when I glimpse one of the children – a tribute – struggling against a crewmember who pushes him down into the ship's hold. Did the child fall to the lower deck? I wonder. Even though part of me wants to race over to see, I stay rooted in place.

"Spell Racer is one of the fastest ships in the world." Captain Dara claims before she turns and bellows, "Cast off and drop sails, you slugs!" Several robed figures scurry forward to unwind the moorings holding Spell Racer to the dock. "Drop sails! Kane - see us out of the harbor."

The captain stands there scrutinizing her crew's work until – once she's finally satisfied – she grabs me by the arm and hauls me over to the trap door that leads into the hull. Part of me wants to resist, just like that little boy did. When Dara pulls me down the ladder, the sound of crying children greets me as I'm pulled past their cell.

"Don't worry about them," Dara says. "They'll be fine once they get accustomed to our ways. Now come on. You'll be staying in my chambers."

Chapter 11

A small window and a couple of candles illuminate Dara's quarters, which consist of little more than a bed separate from the rest of the crew and a desk. Dara pulls her hood back now, which reveals her short dark hair worn in a loose bun. She sits down on the bed and beckons me over next to her with a pat on the mattress.

"I heard you're a witch already," Dara says, seemingly excited to be sitting here with me. All of the bluster and severity of her captaincy is replaced now, and I almost feel like I might be sitting on the bed with Kat.

"Uh...yeah," I say, unsure of myself. "I mean, I've cast a few spells, but not very well. I blinded myself a couple of times."

"Oh, that's normal," Dara says. "It's even worse when an agony spell comes back on you. But that won't be a problem for you for long. Don't worry about it. Mother sends all those spell books out across Zandria, but if you actually use one, there are some really important things left out."

"Wait? Really?" I ask. "Like what?"

"Oh, the main thing is to calm yourself," Dara says. "But don't worry. We'll have plenty of time for spellcasting on the voyage."

"Oh...right," I say. "Especially if you're the captain. You are the captain, right? How did *that* happen?"

"*That?*" Dara asks, bringing some of her severity back. "Are you *questioning* my ability to command this vessel?"

"Oh no, I mean -"

In the next moment, Dara's hand reaches my throat and squeezes. Suddenly, she's speaking into my choking nostril - "I earned my captaincy. *No one* questions that. And if anyone says my mother gave me this post, they can: Eat. My. Steel." With this simple proclamation, she shoves me away so hard that my head bangs the headboard.

Tears come unwelcome to my eyes as I rub the bump.

"Oh," Dara says as though she's made an unwitting mistake. "I forgot how puny Zandrians are."

"I'm not puny!" I cry, wiping the tears from my eyes with a violent brush of my arm.

"Oh, don't worry," Dara says. "We'll toughen you up. We do all the recruits that way. And we'll make extra sure you survive, being that you're the Centenary Sacrifice and everything. You'll skip becoming a 'shift.' That's where most of them die."

"Die...?" I say.

"There's always risks in gaining power," Dara says. "And always dues to pay. But Mother's immortal. And she says someday I can become like my brothers and sisters and be immortal too. You'll probably die. But don't worry. Most people die, so it's not like you'd be any different."

"...oh, uh, right..." I say. "Um, how did your family become immortal?"

"My mother has a pendant," Dara says, "and my brothers and sisters were changed by Notso into Exalted Ones. They're still here with us, all of them."

"And...that person with you," I say, remembering the hooded figure Sunny had called a scarab, "that was one of your siblings?"

"Yes," Dara says. "That's Mira. She's my closest sibling - only about a hundred years old."

"Oh wow," I say. And then - as though we had somehow summoned her just by our conversation - the door opens, and there is Mira with her chimera sitting on her shoulder – now a bird of some kind instead of a monkey. The darkness of the bird's eyes still unsettles me.

"*Hell-o*," Mira says with a harsh and sickly voice from the darkness within the hood. "I hope Dara is making you feel at home." Before I can reply, the bird flies over to the nightstand and stares at me with its eyes that are somehow darker than the tar-like gloop around them. When I look into them, I feel like they will take me somewhere else - somewhere that I definitely do not want to go.

"I...yes," I say, holding very still because of the closeness of the bird.

"You don't have to be afraid of Little Mira," Dara says, holding out her arm for the bird to jump onto.

"*Little* Mira?" I ask.

"That's how we name them," Dara says, "just like the smaller self of their master, though it's pretty difficult whenever they're together. They change shapes to whatever suits them, so there's really no telling them apart unless they're separated."

Even though Little Mira perches on Dara's shoulder, its eyes remain trained on me.

"All this attention is...um...a lot? I mean, I really appreciate you welcoming me here on your ship and helping me get to Witch Marsh, but - if you're *not* going to sacrifice me in the pit - which I couldn't help hearing you tell the High Mister is where you're heading - why all of this? I'm thankful for you taking me to Witch Marsh, but I don't expect to be anyone important there."

"Not important?" Dara asks, and I hope at once that I haven't offended her.

"The Centenary Sacrifice," Mira cuts in with her sickly voice, "is *always* important."

"I mean, I don't think that *I'm* important," I say. "Maybe the others were. Who was the last one...Rollo something?"

"*Rollo Barnes*," Mira spits with palpable contempt.

"What happened to him?" I ask.

"Oh, mother killed him," Dara says, "But don't worry. He didn't have the same appreciation for witch culture that you have. I mean, you're one of us, right?"

"Oh, right," I say, nodding.

"Yes, Rollo," Mira hisses, "was *very* Zandarian." She spits again. "He wanted to make the sacrifice."

"Oh, wow," I say. "I want to be clear. I have absolutely *no* intention of sacrificing myself, there or anywhere else."

"But the Wilder is a crafty one," Mira sneers. "Best to keep our eyes on you." I can't help imagining Mira's eyes deep inside the darkness of her hood, and I almost shiver.

"And Mother's worried about that too," Dara adds, "which is why we'll take the best care of you, and you'll *never* want to have anything to do with that Wilder again."

"Right," I say, nodding. "Now I understand. And on that subject, the boy I was traveling with –"

"– the *Cassock?*" Mira croaks. I imagine the horror on her face - though I still can't see anything under her hood.

"Yes, that one. I was hoping he could –"

"– He has been added to Zandria's tribute," Mira says, "as a *shift*."

I pause a moment before saying, "I guess I don't really understand what that means."

"You will!" Mira cackles before rising and heading towards the door. "Shift! Shift! Shift!"

"My siblings really enjoy shifting," Dara says as the goop bird flies out the door after its master. "They don't need to do it themselves, but they find it fascinating. I know Mira's a bit unusual – especially to a Zandrain, but she's really helpful to have onboard. Her chimera is a much better lookout than Shale in the crow's nest. And those Wilders are sneaky. I've had run-ins with them before, and a chimera can sniff them out miles away and track them."

"And..." I ask with a swallow, "How far away can these chimera go to track down a person?"

"Far," Dara says. "Why?"

"...No reason...," I reply. The eyes of darkness, though, flash in my mind.

"Mother doesn't loan them out much," Dara continues. "Most of the Exalted Ones are her personal guard. It's a shame. They could do so much, but Mother just wants them to protect her all the time."

"Why?" I ask. "I thought she was immortal?"

"Oh, she *is*," Dara says, "and beautiful. But that is the nature of it, isn't it? Other witches covet her power."

"They *do?*" I ask.

"Don't worry," Dara says. "No one who crosses my mother lives long enough to regret it."

"Right," I nod.

"Well, I'd better attend to some things on deck," Dara says. "You know, whip those slugs into line." She squeezes my arm a little too hard, throws her hood back over her head, and stalks out of her quarters, leaving me there to ponder exactly what is going to happen to me.

Chapter 12

Once I finally build up my nerve, I peek out the door to the captain's quarters and find a woman preparing vegetables of some kind with a kettle and a small hearth. There's a flu above her, and the smoke gets sucked up to the outside above. I don't think she notices me, though, which is good, because she's the only person between me and my goal – the cage of tributes on the far side of the ship.

I try to tiptoe, but it's not so easy on a deck that rolls beneath me. I end up stumbling about, but by some miracle, she doesn't notice me. Then I hold a finger to my lips as I approach the children and am greeted by their red and puffy eyes.

"Food," one of them whispers, and it is only now that I remember how hungry I am as well.

"I'm sorry," I say, "I don't have any food."

"What are they going to do with us?" another asks, but I hold my hands open because I don't know that either. Then Aden, whom I actually *am* here to see, steps forward.

He glares at me. "They locked me in a cage," he says under his breath. "These witches are turning out to be just as bad as we heard they were."

"Well," I whisper back angrily, "I'm not sure what you want *me* to do about it. *You* didn't have to come, and the Ministry that *your* father is part of sent them here."

"I see," Aden whispers. "And I suppose the Witchlanders have no responsibility in all of this?"

"Keep your voice down," I say, hushing him while shooting a look over my shoulder at the cooking woman. "Like I said, what can I do about it? It's not like I'm in charge here."

"You're not in a cage, though either, are you?" Aden asks.

"I'm not," I say, "...maybe for the first time. You know, you're just mad that I get to be on top among the witches while you have to see what life's like on the bottom - as an *undesirable*."

With that, I climb the ladder to the deck above, turn and wave a smug goodbye, and try hard to ignore the other faces staring back at me.

As I reach the top deck, I find Dara staring through a spyglass out to some point on the horizon.

Then I hear Mira's grating voice say, "They're two spans to the east in their war canoes."

"Still can't see anything," Dara replies as various other witches go about their business, swabbing the deck and working ropes. "Should we try to catch them?"

"You know what the Queen would say," Mira screeches back.

"That we can't risk our cargo?" Dara asks.

"You remember the last time the Wilders rescued the shifts," Mira says almost tauntingly.

"That was Dorrian," Dara volleys back. "I'm the captain now, and I'm not cowering and skulking back to my mother just because of my cargo. Kane! Set a course for the rocks."

It's only now that Dara turns and sees me. "Shale!" she cries up to the crow's nest. The face of a boy emerges. "Take Ayda and get her dressed in some of my clothes." A boy scurries down, swings from a rope, and lands in front of me, motioning me on without a word.

How old can Shale be? I wonder as I follow him back the way I came - eight, nine? Then I see markings on his neck, and just as I look closer at them, they seem to transpose in my mind to say *Dara's*.

"Hey, Shale," I say as he pulls some clothes out of the closet for me, sizing them by holding them up to me. "What's that mark on your neck?"

He flinches. "I'm Dara's shift," he says.

"What does that mean?" I ask. "Do you work for her?"

He stares at me. Then, without answering my question, he says, "These should fit," and leaves the room just as quickly.

By the time I'm clothed in black robes, I walk out and see the cooking woman ladling out bowls of porridge to the crewmembers.

"Hey, you, girl," the woman calls in a harsh voice. "Come get your rations - I don't have all day." She meets me halfway, shoves a bowl into my hands, and marches off, leaving me to watch the other shipmates eat. They eye me warily.

I realize as I put the first spoonful of porridge in my mouth that I may have been too quick to hope I would find my place easily among the witchlanders. Even if Dara seems friendly in her way, the ship's crew doesn't see me as one of them - maybe because their captain is housing me. I ponder these things as I step back into Dara's quarters with my bowl.

After I finish and bring the bowl back out, I see the cooking woman rankling her spoon on the bars of the tribute's cell before pitching a bucket full of biscuits at them. She laughs scornfully as she watches them grab them up off the floor to shove into their little mouths. Aden stands there watching it all. And I realize after the scramble goes on for a few moments that he won't get any. He's letting the others have it. But then, when a bigger boy grabs a biscuit from a smaller girl, Aden grabs him by the hand and shakes the biscuit free.

"You!" the cooking woman shouts. "We don't tolerate any of that weak-hearted nonsense here. If you take a biscuit, you eat it yourself. Now go on and put that in your gob or no breakfast for the lot of you!"

Warily, Aden picks up the biscuit and puts it in his mouth.

"There you are!" the woman says encouragingly. "We'll get ya sorted out yet!" As she turns back my way, I quickly close myself back into Dara's quarters. Then, with nothing else to do, I lie down on the bed.

As I lay staring at the ceiling above, feeling the ocean roll beneath me, I wonder if this is really what I wanted? It's almost exactly as much as I could have hoped for – and yet not. If this is what I really wanted, why do I still feel so hollow?

Chapter 13

"Hello, Ayda," Sunny says.

I sit up, seemingly back in Kern. There's a wheatfield on my right and a forest on my left, and there, directly before me, is the goofy-looking kid who's been mixed up in this adventure from the start.

"*Sunny!*" I say in alarm. "Where are - how did I -"

"We're in a dream," Sunny explains. "And I'm here to guide you, as always."

"*In my dreams?*" I ask in stark bewilderment.

"Well, I could have boarded the ship," Sunny replies, "but that would have made things complicated, so for now, here I am in your dreams."

"But how do I even know this is real?" I ask. "Or how is this even possible?"

"You're the Centenary," Sunny says, "and I am the Wilder. And dreaming is a very natural thing."

"No," I say with complete certainty. "There is *nothing* natural about meeting someone in their dreams! Besides, I'm not the Centenary anymore. They're not going to sacrifice me. In fact, I'm well on my way to being a witch."

"You're *still* the Centenary," Sunny asserts, "and you can trust me when I tell you that they will try to use you for their own purposes. By the way, how is your brother, Aden?"

"He's *fine*," I say, before realizing the foolishness of my claim. "I mean, he's *alive*. They're making him a 'shift,' whatever that is."

Sunny runs his hand through the heads of grain. "And it doesn't bother you that the Witchlanders practice a form of slavery?" he asks.

This stops me for a moment, but then I find my voice again. "In Zandria, I didn't feel particularly free, either."

"And now the difference is that you get to be the enslaver?" Sunny asks. "Don't you think that perhaps all of this is wrong? What happened to you in Zandria, and what you see now on the ship?"

"Well...I can't stop it!" I cry in exasperation.

"What if you could?" Sunny asks with a smile. "What if you could free those children? Would you?"

"I...yes, I would free them," I say in exasperation.

"You will have a chance to do just that," Sunny says.

"How?"

"When I see you again, I'll explain. Be ready."

With that, he disappears, and I watch as the vision collapses. The wheatfield and the forest are sucked into a single point until I stand in a sea of darkness that winks out as I open my eyes.

Strangely, I find myself staring into an even blacker and more disturbing darkness.

Chapter 14

Mira stands over me.

My eyes pop trying to find definition in the scarab's cavernous hood, but there is none to be found.

"Ahh!...I, hello," I say before Mira steps back.

"He was here," Mira says in her sickly-sweet voice, "wasn't he?"

"Who?" I ask.

"The Wilder!" Mira hisses. It's only now that I find Mira's chimera monkey staring down on me from the headboard with his void-like eyes. I let out a quick scream, startled by his sudden upside-down appearance, before I quickly scramble out of bed and find Dara rising from a hammock, strung up in the room.

"*Mira*, stop scaring our guest!" Dara calls, jumping up out of the hammock with skilled ease.

Mira's attention on me, however, doesn't waver and she holds her dark gaze on me for several more long and agonizing moments before breaking away her gaze and storming out of the room.

"She's always broody," Dara says.

"And are your other siblings like that too?" I ask.

"Yeah," Dara sighs. "They're pretty much all like that."

"Will you be like that?" I ask.

Dara looks at me but doesn't say anything for a few moments. Then she turns away and says, "Being an Exalted One is supposed to be awesome.

Notso takes away all your pain, makes you immortal, invulnerable." Dara shakes her head. "Come on, we'd better get your lessons started before I soften up too much."

I get myself ready, come out, and get a biscuit slapped into my hand by the same cook from last night - Zita, I think, from what the others call her. I take and eat it under the glare of her cold eyes. The rest of the crew gets above deck, and Dara beckons me over to the tribute cage, where I find Aden and several other increasingly hollow faces staring back at me.

"Choose one," Dara says. "Your first shift."

I don't really know anything about shifts or any of these children. There's only one person I do know, so I point to Aden and say, "him."

"You're sure?" Dara asks.

"Why wouldn't I be?" I ask.

"The purpose of a shift," Dara says, "is that when you suffer any hurt or pain, you shift it onto them."

"Really? I ask.

"Really," Dara says with a smile. "Oh, Shale!" she calls. Immediately, the young boy who'd helped get me clothes appears at the ladder from the deck above.

"Shale is one of my shifts," Dara says. "He's the youngest, least senior shift, which means he has to take whatever I throw at him. But one day, if he keeps on, he'll gain seniority. He might rise to the position of navigator, like Kane, or cook, like Zita. Come down here, Shale."

The boy climbs down slowly and stands up straight in front of Dara. He takes deep, measured breaths and looks straight ahead.

"Now, here's a demonstration," Dara says. "Shale has work to do, so nothing too harsh." Dara takes out a knife, pulls the blade up to her own shoulder, and makes a small cut. Then she says a word. I hear that word as "*shift*," but I can tell that those aren't the syllables she has spoken.

And then, like magic, the cut on Dara's shoulder disappears, and when I look over to Shale, I see a red line break open on his shoulder.

"When two powerful witches duel," Dara says, "sometimes hundreds of shifts can die." She must see the horrified look on my face because she adds, "But that doesn't happen very often. And you can lessen the pain by spreading it out over many shifts."

"Shifting pain?" I say uneasily.

"Of course," Dara says. "It's not that different from *causing* pain, is it?"

"I...I guess not," I say.

"That's what being a witch is about," Dara says, "Power. And power comes from being the one inflicting the pain, not being the one receiving it. But the shifts know that if they can take the pain long enough, someday they can be the ones to dish it out. In fact, Shale wears Kane's mark, too. And someday, someone will wear his mark. I don't think you know what an honor it is for you to skip being a shift in witch society. Only a very few people are allowed to do it.""Were you," I ask hesitantly, "a shift?"

"I am my mother's shift and hers alone - that is how I pledge my loyalty to her," Dara says.

"Your mother," I still say hesitantly, "sends you her pain?"

"I'm not a *weakling*," Dara snaps back. "Are you a weakling, Ayda?"

"I'm...*no*," I say a little too quickly.

"Then choose your first shift," she says. "You still want your companion?"

As I look over to the cage, I lock eyes with Aden. It's almost like I can hear a voice in my mind telling me all the reasons my pain should be *his* pain - how he stole the life of privilege I deserved, how he's looked down on me and stood idly by as his friends tormented me.

"Aden," I say.

"Yesss," Mira hisses, appearing behind me seemingly out of nowhere as Dara brings him out of the cage.

"Now," Mira says, "you must mark him with your symbol." She pulls a piece of parchment from her robes and cries, "Draw it there!"

The only thing I can think of is the simple tree I had Mrs. Cartwright tattoo on my ankle, so I draw it, and before I know it, the ship's pilot, Kane, tattoos it directly onto Aden's neck in the most visible place possible. As the tears fall from Aden's face, I realize that perhaps this is a mistake. This mark will stay with him for the rest of his life, and even worse, it will forever close the door to any opportunities in Sandersville. They would never overlook this kind of blemish - a witch symbol on his neck - even if he had no choice in receiving it. With a simple nod, I have dragged him down to my level. I have made him an undesirable.

Anger boils in my veins, but I'm not entirely sure why. Am I angry at him or at myself?

"It's time to cast a spell," Dara says, breaking me from my thoughts.

"Right," I say, shaking my head. She keeps staring at me, and I try to pull myself together. "Um...what spell should I cast? And," I turn away from Aden, "who should I cast it at?"

Dara smiles. "You'll cast your first spell at me," she says. "How else can I assess your strength if I don't feel it?"

Kane, who still packs away his tattooing needles, shoots me a dirty glare.

"And of course," Dara continues, "once I've assessed that strength, I will be shifting the blow to the rest of the crew, who have all pledged their loyalty to me by wearing my mark." Her glare hardens at Kane, who grunts and leaves to go back above deck.

Next, Dara steps forward and hands me a leatherbound spellbook. I can tell at once the quality of the craftsmanship that went into its creation, making it in every possible way the opposite of the cheap rags bound between loose boards that I owned before.

"We'll start with this one," Dara says, pointing to a page entitled, 'How to Beguile Your Enemies.' "Here are the words and the phonetics below to help you sound it out. And it matters that you say the words correctly but not as much as you getting the feeling right inside of you. Keep the person you're casting the spell at in the forefront of your mind and make sure to relax yourself. It's when you tighten up too much that spells rebound. Let's see - what should I try and have you do? How about making me offer you some water? "

"Are you sure?" I ask.

"It's a foolish choice of spells," Mira sneers.

"Oh, shush, Mira," Dara says, waving her sister away as I take the spell book and look over the beautifully hand-written symbols and words. "Don't you remember - I helped train Rodin's ward? I know what I'm doing."

Then she turns back to me. "You see this symbol here," she says, pointing to the top corner of the page. I flinch. It's the same one I put on my thigh. I didn't know it when I tattooed it there, but now I can clearly see that it means 'despicable.'

"This is the symbol from which you draw the power. It's the most important one, so try to say it correctly. Eventually, you will memorize the words and spells, as I did. The more easily you say them and keep your target in your mind, the better the spell will work. And here's another key. You must clear yourself of any sense of empathy. That helps too."

I look at the symbols, which I can now read as though they were any words in the common books we read in the schoolhouse. *I am completely despicable. You should despise me - so I beguile you.*

"These words say-"

"*No*," Dara replies tersely, "I *told* you, the words are *not* the point. The words work. That's the point."

"And you want me to beguile *you?*" I ask.

"I want you to *try* to beguile me," Dara says, ending with a haughty laugh. "Don't get too cocky yet, Ayda. Besides, Mira will help me if I fall too far under your thrall."

I swallow and take a moment to look back at Mira, whose face still remains shrouded in the darkness of her hood. When I look back at the spell book, I don't quite know what comes over me, but I start doodling with my finger invisible lines on the page.

"Hey. What are you doing?" Dara asks.

"Just trying to get a handle on this spell," I say before I take one last deep breath. I don't even really know how I come up with it, but I focus on Dara and start speaking without looking at the spellbook - "*I'm not despicable, you're not despicable. Dara, now we're friends*".

"That sounded pretty good except for some of the Ays and Aww sounds," Dara says. "Now, if you feel any blowback from the spell, which may happen even if your spell is ineffective, that's why you have a...uh, shift. This symbol...this symbol..."

She's pointing to a symbol that means '*share*,' but she stops and shakes her head before a tear suddenly runs down her face. One and then another.

"What..." Dara cries, "What have you done to me! What do you want? You want some water? Here! Have it!" She almost throws the bucket at me and then marches off before screaming back to me, "Go!... Go back to your room!... Please...please go!"

As Dara climbs up to the upper deck, Mira steps forward and shoves Aden in my direction, almost making me spill the bucket's precious, clean water on him.

Even though I can't see into the darkness of her hood, I feel Mira's scowl, but all she says is, "He's yours now - yours to do with as you wish."

"Right," I say, before I pull Aden up and hurry him over to the captain's quarters. He's still clutching his neck, and I almost wish I had some herbs to make him a poultice, but instead I take a cloth, dip it in the bucket, and hand it to him.

I feel like apologizing to him, but the words get stuck in my mouth. And my other thoughts soon crowd out this sympathy. How did I even do what I just did? Did I just get lucky? What will happen the next time I do a spell?

Aden closes the door behind us. He looks at me but doesn't say a word before he sits down and stares at the deck floor. He stays that way for quite some time, and I still don't have any words to give him. What can he say now that he's my slave?

Chapter 15

"Hello, Ayda," Sunny says.

I look around myself. I'm still in the captain's quarters on *Spell Racer*, but I must have nodded off. The colors are too full, the light too sweet, the air too clean.

"Hello...?" I say back. "What are you doing here?"

"Guiding you, of course. Come with me," Sunny says as he waves me out into the main below-deck area. "You have an important decision to make," Sunny continues. "Wilders will soon attack this ship to free the Zandrians who are enslaved as tributes. Look here," he points, showing me a leather pouch. It's nailed to the cabinet where Zita keeps her cookware. "This is where the key to the cage is hidden."

I gulp a swallow. "What do you want me to do about that?" I ask.

"When you hear the attack, unlock the door," Sunny says, and a haze immediately spreads everywhere.

"Wait!" I cry. "What happens after that?"

"The tributes escape," he says matter-of-factly.

"But...what about me?"

"What about you?" Sunny asks in reply, fading faster and faster. "Didn't you choose this path? To go to Witch March? There's still a choice, even now. Unlock the door."

And then Sunny is gone, and I wake with a start.

Aden looks over from where he's still sitting on the floor with his pouty face. Part of me wants to tell him it's not that bad, but *I'm* not the slave.

"You know," I say, suddenly getting an idea, "what would you think about getting rescued from here?"

This heightens Aden's attention. "What do you mean?" he asks cautiously.

"I mean that the Wildrians might attack the ship, and you could, you know, escape. Say that happened - would that make you feel better?"

Aden shakes his head in disbelief. "...I *guess.*" And then, hope seems to come into his eyes, but then he shakes his head. "You would still be here. And now I don't know what to think anymore. When Da sent me off to protect you, I thought I'd bring you back to Kern, and then...then I thought things would go back to how they were, but..."

"...things will never be how they were," I say, finishing for him.

"No," Aden says. "Nothing will ever be the same. And now it seems like there are only two outcomes - you get sacrificed, or you become a witch. And if you're a witch, I have to be your slave. I've been trying my best to keep you from getting sacrificed..."

"...but you don't want to be my slave," I finish for him. "Aden, you should wear a high collar and just go home."

"You should go too," Aden says.

"You don't get it," I reply. "I don't *have* a home anymore." As I say this, I realize more and more that it's true. I can never go back to Ma's hut or school. The ministry will never stop hunting me if I ever return to Zandria. Which only leaves Witch Marsh, doesn't it?

But now, just as I'm thinking these thoughts, I hear a commotion above, and I rush out of the quarters.

"Crank the ballista!" Dara shouts.

Scrambling feet rush above me. I stare up at the sky through the hole to the top deck when Zita scrambles past me up the ladder. A thud and a whizzing sound ring up above, and right when Zita blocks out the sky, I remember the key.

"Aden!" I call back to where he stands in the doorway to the captain's quarters. "Come on."

"What's going on?" he asks.

"Just come on," I say, rushing to where Zita was cooking only moments before, and there, right where Sunny showed me in the vision, I find the key to the cell. All the tributes look around in alarm at the sounds coming from outside.

"Water," one of the tributes says as I approach with the key.

"Aden, bring water," I say. I unlock the door while Aden rushes back to the water barrel and scoops out a bucket full. Soon, the poor orphans are pushing to get their mouths to the rim.

"Slow down," I say as I edge closer to the ladder. "I'm going to go up to see how things are going. I'll call down when it's time for you to come up." Aden nods.

When I crawl up onto the main deck, though, it seems that the crew has fended off the war canoes. As I stand, I can see the closest one sinking with a huge harpoon stuck through it.

"Hurry!" Mira screeches. "Hit them with agonizing pains so that they drown."

"Follow them!" Dara cries as the ship goes further into the rocks. "I want to take them alive – we need shifts, not corpses!"

I panic. *There's enough time to fix this*, I think, as I try to slow my breathing. I can convince all the tributes to get back into their cage. I can make up some story about why one of the barrels is short of water.

Cautiously, I edge over to the railing and look down at the sinking canoe and the Wilders swimming away. Kane fires the ballista at one of the swimmers, but the large shaft just barely misses to one side. Then Kane twirls right around and looks me straight in the eyes. "Hand me that bolt!" he shouts, pointing to the spears.

I begin to back away when Kane rushes to shove me out of his way and grab the next spear. He sweeps past me and begins cranking the ballista himself over the bodies of his crewmates, who have strange darts sticking out of their bodies. I don't stay to watch him fire the contraption again.

Quick – I think – *I need to get back below deck!* But I trip over Shale's prone, dart-stuck body, and go sprawling across the deck.

Facedown on the cold boards I feel a *tap, tap* on my shoulder. "Need a hand?" a voice asks.

My heart falters as a hand grasps my shoulder. Tears come to my eyes. I turn around expecting Kane or Zita, but to my surprise I find –

"Sunny?"

"Of course," Sunny replies. He's wet - completely wet, and his hair is completely flat with water. Did he come out of the water? He smiles and says, "Things are about to get good."

He points up to the cliffs above us where a large cohort of Wildrian warriors crouches. Suddenly, these people clad in tropical fabrics are swinging down onto the ship. They shoot darts from tubes at their belts. Kane falls first, then another sailor.

"Ambush!" Dara cries. "About face - don't let them take you alive!" Dara raises her sword and charges towards the nearest Wildrian, stabbing for a near miss before a string of words launches a strange projectile out of her, bringing a large Wildrian writhing to his knees before a dart sprouts from her neck, and she goes down.

And here I am in the middle of all this upheaval, standing as still as possible while Sunny puts a reassuring hand on my shoulder.

In moments, all of the crew have been taken out by the darts, and those Wildrians who were shaking in agony or blinded seem to have shaken it off a lot faster than I shook off my blindness. And that's when Mira sits straight up and pulls the darts out from her side, tossing them away like some sort of trash.

"*You will not take her!*" Mira screeches.

"She is free to choose," Sunny replies.

"*She has already chosen!*" Mira cries. "Do you not *know* of the marks on her body wrought by her own hand?!"

"By freeing the tributes," Sunny says calmly, even as he eyes a boy's head poking up through the deck hatch, "she has made a new choice. Her next choice is free to her as well - to continue with you to Witch Marsh or to come with us to the island of Wildria."

Aden and the tributes now stand on deck. Will they be able to escape to Wildria if I choose to go on to Witch Marsh? I have never heard much about Wildria except that it is a rocky island, the largest and furthest of the northeastern archipelago, but however rocky it is, I imagine it must be better than living as a shift.

"I will go to Wildria," I say to the quick cheers of the tributes.

"Then it's settled," Sunny says.

"Nothing is settled," Mira screams. "*Nothing!*"

With a shriek, Mira throws her hood back to reveal a formless face covered in the same dark and gloopy tarlike substance that makes up her chimera - which now rushes over from a corner of the deck and jumps straight into her face, merging with the other goo. From there, the tar seems to separate from Mira altogether before forming what appears to be a much larger chimera - a gigantic bat with wings several spans long and sporting cruelly twisted claws on its toes. Then, with one forward flap, the bat pounces and curls its feet around me, ripping me into the air as it flaps away.

My world goes sideways and upside down - I would scream except the claws grasp me so tightly that I can barely breathe. Soon, I see the rocky peninsula below us getting smaller and smaller.

"Sunny," I rasp. "Aden..."

In another moment, something else appears in the sky. It's so small at first, and upside down, that I can barely tell what it might be. But moment by moment it grows in my sight until I see the spikes and wings of a creature I can't believe - a winged rock dragon. Until this moment, I thought they only lived in legends. And even more surprising - Sunny rides on its back.

The rock dragon closes in on the giant bat chimera, but I have no idea how Sunny plans to free me from the dark beast's grasp. Then I hear Sunny's voice boom like thunder, "*You **will** respect her choice*."

In the next moment, Sunny leaps from the rock dragon onto the goop bat's back, and I hear a sizzling, popping sound as the goop bat that was Mira screeches in a pitch so high that I wish I could reach my ears to close them.

Then, when I finally *can* reach my ears, I'm also falling. The sound of rushing wind replaces the screech, and the fear of splatting on the rocks below fills me so completely that I lose consciousness for a moment before coming back to myself in the grasp of another clawed foot, this time the rock dragon's. Having now experienced flying in the grasp of two giant beasts, I immediately prefer the second. My bruised ribcage can at least rest easy now.

"Sunny!" I call, trying to reach him on top of the dragon. He pokes his head out over the rock dragon's shoulder and smiles down at me. Then he points below, drawing my attention to Spell Racer still sitting in the water near the rock cliff.

We glide over the water and come so close that we almost hit the ship's mast before great flapping strokes by the dragon bring us to a near stop, before the gigantic foot releases me gently into the sea. When I surface, the rock dragon is gone, and I find Sunny treading water next to me, his poofy hair shrunken once again.

Ropes are thrown over to Sunny, and he helps me tie a rope under my arms, which the Wildrians use to pull me back up onto the deck, where I find Dara waking up from the dart.

"Ayda," Dara calls, looking around as she comes out of her stupor. Still soaking wet, I move towards her but am stopped by the husk that was once Mira, which immediately catches Dara's attention as well. Without her hood, the see-through black fabric over her face shows something more skeletal than flesh.

"My sister - you've killed her!" Dara shouts. I am about to protest this accusation when she turns and points her finger at Sunny. "You're nothing but a killer!"

Sunny barely reacts, even when she moves to hit him. He catches Dara by the wrist - one first, then the other - and waits for her to stop, pushing her away from himself when she goes to knee him.

"Your sister," Sunny says solemnly, "she died a long time ago at the hands of Notso - shortly after your mother killed Rollo. The truth is that your mother didn't need your sister anymore after Rollo died. In fact, she only has children when she hopes to use them to influence the Centenary Sacrifice, or hadn't you guessed? Or do you think it is a coincidence that you are so close in age to Ayda? And what do you think will happen to you if Ayda dies?"

"My sister was exalted," Dara cries, "just like I will be. And Ayda will be my sister witch. We will dance over your bones, Wilder, and spit on them! *As wretchedness brings agony to my soul, so your body will writhe in agony!"*

Then the same dark burst comes out from Dara that I saw before, but when the hex hits Sunny, he does not seem affected by it at all. In fact, it disappears entirely. In the next moment, several Wildrians tackle Dara, gag her with a cloth, and tie her hands behind her back. She struggles, but the Wildrians are stronger.

"Wilder," a large man says as he approaches Sunny. He goes down on a knee for a full bow. "What shall we do with the captives?"

"Put them in the rowboat," Sunny replies, "all except for the daughter of Jezrella. Put her in the cell that held the Zandrian Tributes. Then I will tell you how to set the sails. We are taking this ship to Wildria."

I watch helplessly as they drag Dara away. Did I choose this? Is this new destination really any better than Witch Marsh?

Chapter 16

After we clear the rocks, we find the wind blowing from the direction we want to go, forcing us to tack left and right to make any progress. I feel like the ship is almost as confused about which way to go as I am. I go to the bow to keep out of the way of the mast swinging back and forth at every turning and let the wind blow through my hair

The Wildrians, meanwhile, feed the tributes, who are justifiably hungry. I look beside us and realize that several war canoes have joined us, some with fresh scars from the harpoons shot from the Spell Racer. Their small sails and outriggers keep them racing along with the wind.

When we stop to tack back right, one of the canoes comes up beside us and ropes are lowered to pull two Wildrian youths up onto the ship while two other warriors whose own canoe had been sunk are lowered down to take their pace. These two soon make their way over to me to make my acquaintance, probably because they are near my age.

"We're twins," the girl says. "I'm Nina, and this is Naru." They are tall and lithe and have tan skin, and while I can tell that they aren't quite as dark as Sunny, they are darker than I am. Their clothing is similar to Sunny's, but like the other warriors, they have what looks like hardened bark plates strapped on for armor - something Nina actually starts removing.

"So you're the centenary?" the boy asks, just as curious about me as I am about them.

"That's right," I say as Aden joins us.

"Are you going to do it? Are you actually going to sacrifice yourself?"

"*Naru!*" the girl scolds.

I would answer, but I feel paralyzed. I look at Aden, then back to Naru. Finally, I say, "No. I don't think so."

"– *What?*" Naru exclaims. Anger wells up inside of him. "*I* would do it! If that's what it took to end all of this, I would go right now and do it!"

"Naru! For Sandor's sake. She's not doing it. We'll just go on as we always have. Besides, no one said anything about the war ending if the sacrifice is made."

"Well, it has to do *something*," Naru says before storming off to the other side of the ship.

"Don't mind him," Nina says comforting.

"Right," I say, wondering how many other Wildrians will feel like Naru. Maybe going to Wildria isn't a great idea after all. Maybe I should have flown off with the giant goop bat.

"I guess you're the Centenary's companion?" Nina asks Aden.

"I'm her brother," Aden replies. "But yes, I guess I am."

"How do you feel about becoming a Wilder?" Nina asks.

"I, uh," Aden starts, "never thought of it before."

"I'm just asking," Nina says, "because there's a long history of the centenary's companions taking refuge in Wildria after...you know, *after*."

"After I die?" I ask.

Nina seems lost for words until she says, "I'm sorry."

"No, I get it," I say. "There's no time like now for recruiting. Aden, I hope you're very happy in Wildria."

"Well, I can't really go back home now, can I?" he asks, his voice barbed in my direction, probably for the tattoo I forced him to take on his neck.

"The witch queen usually tries to kill the Centenary's companions afterwards," Nina says. "That's why they usually take refuge in Wildria."

"*Oh*," Aden says.

"It's alright," Nina says, encouraging. "You'll love it in Wildria!"

"Right," Aden says before he steps away from Nina to grab the railing. He looks dismally out at the horizon, now feeling the full weight of our impending future.

"Well, at least you get to *live* somewhere," I call after Aden, even as I turn to go to the other side of the ship. No one in Zandria wants to go to the island of Wildria. Some people say it's full of savages. As someone regularly called a witch, I've always doubted that assertion. Of course, now I *am* a witch, so who can say? Even still, savages or not, I'm not excited to journey to a rocky and desolate island, especially if I'm going to be crushed under the weight of their expectations.

"Ayda!" a voice calls from the ladder to the deck below.

"Sunny?" I call as I turn around.

Sunny beckons me from the ladder. "Your friend is asking for you," he says.

I nod and go with him, climbing down the ladder to find Dara in the cell that once held the tributes.

There she is, murder in her eyes, now looking at me.

"Hi," I say.

Dara doesn't respond right away. Her hood is back, and her gag has been loosened so that it rests just below her chin. One of the Wildrians stands with a blow gun at the ready. I assume he is to shoot her with it if she begins to recite a spell.

"Hi there," Dara says back. "You're not in here with me, so I'm guessing that the Wildrians have offered you something."

"For now," I say, "I am traveling with them to Wildria."

"My mother will come for me," Dara says, "and she will come for you. I was sure that if I brought you to her, she would allow you to live. But now, I don't know what will happen."

"Everyone wants me to die," I say, shaking my head. "Would she really kill me?"

Dara nods. "The Witch Queen is many things, but merciful is not one of them."

I nod. There it goes, then - my dream to fit in as a witch in Witch Marsh. But my mind twirls. Who's to say I wasn't taken hostage as well as Dara? Only Dara herself. Is Wildria really the place I want to go, or do I still want to go to Witch Marsh? For the moment, I've committed to going to Wildria, but after?

Sunny looks at me and asks, "Do you want to tell me what you're thinking?""Definitely not," I reply. "Will Jezrella be able to get us?"

"That depends," Sunny says. "Do you want to be gotten?"

I huff. Is Aden right - is Sunny some sort of wizard? Can he hear my thoughts?

"I'm not answering that," I say. "You're frustrating. Do you know that?"

"Just frustrating enough to push you in the right direction I hope," Sunny says with his contagious smile. I'm immune to that contagion though.

"Well, why don't you do something actually helpful," I ask, "like letting my friend out of this cell? The Wildrians do anything you say, don't they?"

"They do better than anyone else," Sunny says. "As for letting Dara out, it's hard to trust someone who practices witchcraft. You never know when they might hex you. When a witch is around, you can't let your guard down for a moment. It's a draining existence, second-guessing every person's motives, never knowing who is going to strike or when. Is that really how you want to live?"

I'm about to tell him that maybe it is, but I notice now that he's not talking to me. He's talking to Dara, and there's a strange look of uncertainty on her face.

"Only when you lay down your fear will you truly be free," Sunny says.

"Wait," I say. "Is that fair? Dara's a captive here. Why shouldn't she be afraid?"

"She's not afraid of us," Sunny says. He then turns to the bulky Wildrian with the blow gun. "Let the girl go free. She will now be counted as a companion of the Centenary."

Dara stares at him, even as the guard nods and opens the cell door. She finally breaks eye contact and steps out, looking around almost as if she's lost.

"Aren't you afraid I'm going to hex someone?" Dara asks, seemingly ready to step back in the cell.

Sunny turns back to her. "No," he says. "And I'm not afraid of your mother either. And I'm not afraid to die."

"You can't die," Dara says. "My mother says she's stabbed you many times, and here you still are. Of course, *you're* not afraid of death!"

"I can die," Sunny says, "but not at the hands of any witch." He smiles then and says. "It's time for some fresh air."

Chapter 17

Everyone's eyes immediately lock onto Dara when she comes up behind me through the hatch to the main deck. The raised blowguns are only stilled by Sunny's raised hands. "She is under my protection," Sunny says before walking up to the ship's bow - apparently to commune with nature or something, leaving me with Dara as Aden, Nina, and Naru approach.

I think Nina might say something, but whatever it was gets stuck in her mouth, and we find ourselves in an awkward silence that Dara finally breaks when she proclaims, "I'm *still* a prisoner."

"But *not* in a cell," Naru says.

"Sunny let her out," I say, taking a step forward.

"You know I've been hearing Sunny this, Sunny that, all my life," Naru replies, "but that's about the stupidest idea I've ever heard of."

"Shut up, Naru," Nina says. "If Sunny says she's alright out of the cell, she's alright to be out of the cell."

"Oh yeah?" Naru says, closing the distance between him and Dara. "Maybe she's about to hex me right now. Is that what you want, *witch?*"

"Stop it!" I cry.

"Did her witches stop when they killed Garro?" Naru asks. "Or when they took Little Fox for their slave camp?"

"Naru, *stop*," Nina says.

"*No*," Naru says, "I'm not going to stop!"

Just as he moves to push Dara, I speak, *"As my soul burns with agony, so your hair will burn with fire."* I feel the pulse shoot out of me, and before my eyes, Naru's long black hair bursts into flame.

Naru screams as my thigh burns with shooting pains, and my legs buckle before I go down on one knee.

Suddenly, Sunny is there putting his hand directly on Naru's flaming head. The fire's gone in the next instant. All is well, I think, but then I watch as a large clump of Sunny's poofy curls fall out. One clump and then another clump. His scalp looks red, ready to bubble and boil. Every last poof falls to the deck, and there, standing before me are two bald boys.

Naru looks shaken. He holds the ashen dome of his head and steps back before pointing at me. "Witch. The Centenary's a witch!"

"Put him in the cell," Sunny says to Chief Sorru.

"What?" Naru yells. "It's them – they should be in the cells!"

"What about her?" the large man asks, pointing to me.

"Put her into the cell as well," Sunny says.

"Wait," Naru says. "No – she'll kill me!"

"She won't," Sunny says, turning to Naru. "If she wanted to kill you, Naru son of Isha and Corru, you would be dead. And I assume you know the punishment for killing the Centenary…?"

"…yes…" Naru says.

"Yes…?" Sunny continues.

"…banishment," Naru finishes. Sunny nods, and they pull Naru away as his crisped and burnt hair blows around on the deck.

"I've never heard that spell before," Dara says as they pull Naru below. I shrug my shoulders. What can I say? That the words just came to me?

When I turn back around, I can't help focusing on Sunny's now barren and scalded scalp. "You know," I say, "I can make a salve for that if you have the ingredients."

Sunny turns to me and smiles. "When we arrive in Wildria, I might take you up on that. But for now, you must go."

"I was trying to –"

"– To protect your friend. I know…" Sunny says, raising a hand to cut me short. "You desire justice. You want to protect the people you love. But the tools of Notso can never accomplish the work of Sandor. It will always end up just like this," he says, pointing to his head.

"I'm sorry," I say as Chief Sorru takes me to the hatch to go below.

"I forgive you," Sunny calls. Then he smiles. "And please, go easy on Naru."

***

So here we sit – one of us on either side of the cage. Neither of us speaks. Instead, we alternate between glaring at each other and looking away.

After several minutes I ask, "How much longer until we get there?"

Naru looks up, surprised to hear me speak. He continues to glare for a few moments before he says, "It shouldn't be much longer now. An hour or two at the most."

"Dara's my friend," I say, deciding to continuing breaking the silence. "And you were being a jerk."

"You're friend's a witch," Naru says back.

"Yeah," I say, "so what? I guess I'm a witch too."

"Witches are evil," Nau says. "They should all die!"

"Well, maybe small-minded jerks should die too!" I say.

Naru flinches into a defensive position with his hands before him, waiting for whatever terrible thing I might to do him, which stops me cold.

He's afraid I'm going to hurt him. And I *have* hurt him. I lower myself back to the ground, now at a loss again for what to say.

We sit again in the cell, staring at one another as the ship lolls beneath us.

"I was tired of being powerless," I finally say.

I feel the symbol for agony on my thigh, where it still burns with tenderness. The pain needles me, and there in the back of my mind, the bud of an idea blossoms. It says *Why suffer? Why endure misery? Just say the word and the pain will go. Say the word, and it will go elsewhere. Shouldn't your brother share in this pain?*

Aden still wears my symbol on his neck. He could share this pain. And the desire to shift it to him rises and rises until I give a small cry and push the thought away as best as I can. And here I am - pained and desolate - as sadness falls on me like a giant wave, mixing me all about as though I'm mixed up in its violent surf. I can't help feeling now that the path I chose was a great mistake, and I can't undo it.

I try desperately to hold back the tears that are welling up in my eyes because I don't want Naru to see them, but they come flowing out anyway. And – oh, that makes me angry! I scowl at him, but when he takes up another defensive posture, I turn around so that I can cry by myself - as much as that's possible.

"Naru, what did you do!" Nina cries at him as she comes down the ladder.

"Nothing!" Naru cries back.

"Aden, get down here!" Nina cries. "Your sister's crying!"

Make it stop, I think. Make them all go away. Save me from their pity. My mouth opens. Words are right there on the tip of my tongue when Aden reaches my hand.

"Hey," Aden says. "I'm here. It will be alright. His hair will grow back."

I nod, afraid to tell him that my doubts, pain, and anger are so much deeper than the loss of Naru's hair.

"I know you," Aden says. "You'll fight anyone if you think it's right. But we're here. You don't have to be alone."

Then I see the spiderweb-like tattoos on Dara's hand as she reaches for mine through the cell bars, too. I look up. Here they are, and a strange feeling comes over me - one I barely recognize through the tears.

I have friends.

Chapter 18

Naru and I are released when we dock at Wildria. As I reach the main deck, I look out for the first time over a city unlike any I've seen. It doesn't have Hook Swallow's rows upon rows of buildings built from wood planks, bricks, and mortar. Instead, I find myself looking at the side of a mountain full of windows and doors that I assume lead into dwellings within. The fact that many of the windows have plants growing in them makes the scene that much more surreal, like a garden growing up the side of a cliff.

"It's solidified volcanic ash," Chief Sorru says. "It covers the whole of the mountain. My ancestors have been carving homes into it for generations."

"Volcanic?" Aden asks, appearing at my shoulder. "Nothing I read about the Wildrian Archipelago mentioned anything about volcanic activity."

"No?" Chief Sorru asks. "Well, that's not surprising - not many Zandrians make it out this way. Or should I say - not many leave."

"...uh, right..." Aden says.

"Don't worry," the chief says, giving a hearty laugh as he slaps Aden good-naturedly on the back. "It is all as Sandor wills!" The back slapping, however, appears to have forced all the air out of my brother's lungs as he coughs to catch his breath. Chief Sorru doesn't seem to notice. "As for the Dragon's Mouth," Sorru says, "it hasn't erupted for many, many years."

Aden, far from being deterred, strikes with another question while *my* attention catches on Dara, who stares out from the railing at an island nation that remains her enemy.

"I don't belong here," Dara says as I join her.

"I know the feeling," I say. "But if Sunny says you're with me, you should be fine."

"Should be," Dara says. "How many others do you think there are here like Naru? My tattoos will be the only thing they see about me. How many others will want revenge?"

"Even if some of us want revenge," Nina says, "we will not kill you in your sleep. That would be shameful. Our darts only induce sleep. We do not kill."

"The Holy Writs of Sandor," I say, "*Don't kill.*"

"You follow all these writs?" Dara asks.

"We try," Nina replies.

Dara's face remains unreadable, but then I see Naru watching from a distance. Aden continues peppering Sorru with questions, but as soon as the gangplank is opened, Naru rushes across, seemingly ready to escape our company.

"Come," Sorru calls to me. "You will all stay in my dwelling."

"Where's Sunny?" I ask as I move down the gangplank.

"In the time I have known the Wilder," Sorru says, "I have learned not to worry about his whereabouts. He is here. He's there. He appears. He disappears. But always he's exactly where he needs to be right when he needs to be there."

"Did he leave?" I ask as we walk into the caves.

"I doubt it," Sorru says. "He asked to speak with you after we get you settled, you and your companions."

I just nod because I can't really tell what I think about Sunny anymore.

As we continue into Wildria, I try to take in what I can about these dwellings. They are mostly carved from the rock, but they are also augmented here and there with wood paneling or brick fireplaces. Mirrors bounce light into the rooms, but the deeper we go, the more oil lamps I see as well.

When we finally arrive at Sorru's dwelling, he introduces me to his wife, Deyla, who shows me to Nina's room and brings Dara there as well to stay. Aden, meanwhile, goes to Naru's room across the hall.

I look down at the bedroll spread on the floor for me and try to settle into the idea of sleeping here tonight, but I can't help feeling like this is a tomb. All my life, I had the sun and moon and stars just a window flap away, but now the outside feels like it's a world away. And what if the lantern goes out? I chide myself for my worries, especially after being blinded, but being trapped in stone still makes me feel uneasy.

"You must give me your clothing," Deyla says when she comes in. "It's no good. We will get you new. Come, give me – give me – give me."

Deyla grabs Dara by the robe and looks like she's about to wrestle Dara to the floor as the witch tires to desperately to pull herself free and escape the older woman's grasp. Finally she rolls out of reach and shouts – "I'm not wearing your grass skirts!" – as she scrambles around the room ahead of her pursuers.

I, meanwhile, watch in idle amusement as I receive my new clothes without protest and drop my witch's robe as easily as a cat yawns. When Deyla finally succeeds in stripping Dara of her robe, I say, "They're just clothes, Dara. Besides, we'll fit in much better with these."

"*You'll* fit in better," Dara says. "I will still have *these* –" she says pointing at her face "– for everyone to see!"

Nina walks in with an outfit. "My aunt says you have to wear this," she tells Dara. "And if you don't, that I should wrestle you to the ground and make you." Nina waits for a moment before smiling innocently. "So, which will it be?"

Dara's frown deepens, but she snatches the outfit out of Nina's hands.

"When you're done dressing," Nina calls behind her, "come out to the main room. Sunny's waiting."

Dara scowls, but I can't tell if it's for her new clothes or having to listen to Sunny.

The common room is a cavernous space larger than my Ma's entire hut, filled with lounging cushions, tables, chairs, a cooking hearth, and some sort of shaft in the ceiling up to the world outside with mirrors somehow reflecting light into a glass or crystal fixture that refracts and spreads the light all throughout the room. There, under that fixture, sits Sunny.

"Welcome," Sunny says. "Come, sit."

"The Centenary will decide whether she sits or not," Dara says defiantly. I shoot her a glare and go sit on one of the cushions. Harumphing, Dara joins me. Aden sits on my other side. Nina and Naru attend as well, with Sorru and Deyla behind.

"Ayda," Sunny says, "when your Ministers in Zandria taught you the story of Mother and Father and Sandor and Notso, there's one key detail they left out. That morning, when Mother and Father decided to walk with Notso, Notso stole words of creation that had been woven around your Great Parents – the words beauty, love, worth, ability, wholeness, true sight, and life. He took those words, twisted them, and made the first spells. Later, one of the grandchildren of Mother and Father, a girl named Shana, became the first witch."

"*Wait!*" Aden cries. "Hold on. That can't be right. I thought Shana was the first sacrifice to Notso!"

"Shana -" Sunny continues, "came to the altar in the pit where Notso is bound. If she had laid herself down for sacrifice on the altar, atonement would have been made, the words of creation would have been taken back from Notso, and all the witch spells would have been broken. As it was, Notso convinced Shana instead to join him as the first witch, and she renamed herself Jezrella. And so it has been with every sacrifice sent to Notso's pit. He has either deceived them into joining the witches who worship him, or his followers have killed them before they could make it to the altar. Despite what the Ministers in Zandria contend, no one has ever been sacrificed in the pit for atonement."

"And let me guess," I say, "I'm supposed to be the first."

"Yes," Sunny says.

"And let's say I agree," I say, "what's to say Jezrella won't kill me before I get there to be sacrificed, like Rollo?"

"You will succeed," Sunny says.

"Did you tell Rollo he'd succeed too?" I ask.

"No," Sunny replies. "I told Rollo that if he persevered and resisted Notso's temptations, he would play an instrumental role in defeating Notso."

"And he believed you?" I ask.

"Yes," Sunny replies.

"And now he's dead," I say.

"Rollo *will* play an instrumental role in defeating Notso," Sunny says definitively.

"You just have all the answers," I say. "You're just so sure of yourself. But I'm the one who's going to die!"

"I don't expect you to understand yet," Sunny says. "You don't know what death is, nor do you know what life is. When Notso took the words of power from Mother and Father, he took the word for life and fashioned it into an amulet that he gave to Jezrella to wear. But as with all things Notso does, it is a perversion. Jezrella's body has lived for ages and ages, even as her spirit has withered."

I glance over at Dara to see her reaction to Sunny's words about her mother, but she just stares grimly on until finally saying, "You know she'll come after us, don't you?"

Sunny nods. "Yes."

"My mother always gets what she wants," Dara says. "And when she doesn't..." The threat hangs in the air. "You let my crew go in canoes, and they will have made it to Fort Dagger by now. And the chimeras will be searching the sea routes. It won't take them long to conclude that Ayda is here. And when my mother comes here..."

"Then the barrier reefs will protect us," Sorru interjects. "And we will fight."

"You will fight," Dara says, "and you will die. My mother will kill every last one of you to get what she wants."

I look at Sunny. He looks at me. "Do you trust me?" Sunny asks. He looks around at all of us. "Do all of you trust me? No one will die. Jezrella will take you on a journey to Witch Marsh. I will be at the Pit, waiting for you."

"Then why did we come here?" I ask.

"You'll see," Sunny says.

Chapter 19

Deyla serves us freshly caught fish for dinner - and it's better fish than I've ever eaten in my life, but I struggle to enjoy it as Sunny's words loop around continuously in my head. It appears that I'm not the only one. Ayden asks Dara question after question about the capabilities of the Witchlander navy, but Dara says very little, trying to glare him into silence, but she doesn't succeed. How many ships are in the navy? - enough. Could they cross a barrier reef? - their canoes could. Could the Wildrians really suffer no casualties? -no.

When I've finally had enough of their conversation, I get up and excuse myself from the table.

I leave Sorru's dwelling. I know it's not the best idea, but I don't really care at the moment, and I just begin wandering the tunnels, quickly losing any sense of direction. I begin to see people. Many of them stare at me. Some point. But I keep going. A couple of times, I accidentally enter people's homes. I apologize and leave.

In a few more turns, I come to a tunnel door that leads me out into the open – an open I didn't expect. My jaw drops in wonder at this sight – a green, lush, and verdant landscape opens up before me like some form of paradise. I look around in utter bewilderment until I find walls far and near and understand that I have somehow found my way into the cone of the volcano. I had assumed this would be a desolate pit, but I was wrong. Row upon row of crops and fruit trees stretch out before me in the volcanic soil. And there in the middle, I find that a pond occupies the center of the crater, around which vents steam up into the colorful sky as the sun winks away beyond the far crater wall.

And I'm soaking in all this beauty before me when the crunch of a shoe jars me out of the moment.

"*Naru*," I cry as I spot him, instinctively backing away from him. "*What are you doing here?*"

"I...I followed you," Naru says. His freshly bald head looms large in my sight.

"You followed me?" I ask, backing away further. "...*why?*"

"My uncle," Naru says, "he asked me to keep an eye on you."

"Does it look like I need to be watched like a toddler?" I ask.

Naru grunts in response. "No. Of course not. I'm sure you can find your way back. I'll leave you to your walk then. Good evening."

"Wait!" I cry. Naru stops and turns back around.

"I...I'm sorry," I say. "I'm sorry I burnt off your hair."

Naru nods. "Well. I'm sorry I threatened your friend," he says.

"And maybe I don't know where I am, or where I'm going."

"Well, fortunate for you, I'm a navigator," Naru says. "I have a sense for it. I can find my way anywhere in all of Landria."

"All of Landria?" I ask.

"It's true," Naru insists.

"What about Nina - is she a navigator?" I ask.

"No," Naru says. "She's studying as a chemist and herbalist. She makes concoctions. Measures poisons for our darts."

"I thought you were a warrior," I say.

"We're *all* warriors," Naru replies. "But we specialize. Even if it's something like agriculture. And then there are also overlapping fields. Navigators are also foragers. We bring back resources and supplies for the people.

Our parents were some of the best. They specialized in Witch Marsh...until they didn't come back..."

Naru is always intense, a boy with fire inside him, but at this moment it seems like his fire has smoldered out.

I pause, struggling to find the right thing to say. "I'm sure they would be proud of you," I say haltingly. "I mean, they will be when they return. Or you find them. I mean, I'm going to Witch Marsh. If you come with me, maybe we'll find them together."

"Maybe," Naru says. "Nina keeps saying we will, but I don't know..."

So here I am at a loss for what to do. "You know," I say, suddenly hoping to lighten things up some, "I really can't believe you're one of those Wilders who treks all over Landria. Kat says she saw one of you out in the woods one time, but I didn't believe her."

"Oh, yeah," Naru grins, regaining a little bit of his old manner. "We try to go unnoticed. And we don't like the outside world to know about the fertile crater by the way, either. Uncle Sorru says that it's part of the reason everyone leaves us alone - because they think there's nothing out here worth having."

I nod.

"But Sunny says that someday we won't have to stay hidden any longer," Naru says.

"He said that?" I ask.

"Not here," Naru says. "Not now. Long ago."

"Sometimes I forget that he's that old," I say.

Twilight has come upon us. Here I am out with a boy as the stars twinkle down from the sky. What would Ma think?

"Maybe we should go," I say.

"Come on," Naru says. "I'll take you back."

I follow Naru back into the caves. Turn after turn, I realize that I am completely at the mercy of his sense of direction, but soon enough, I begin noticing markings that probably are showing him the way - but even still.

"Thank you," I say as we walk back into the common room where Chief Sorru and Deyla still sit.

Dara glares in Naru's direction from Nina's room.

"I just went for a walk," I say. "Naru brought me back."

"That's one of the things my brother's good for," Nina says, "fetching things."

"Well, *I* didn't know where you were," Dara says with a hint of accusation in her voice.

"I'm...*sorry*," I say, biting the word as it comes out uncertainly. "It's all a lot. I mean, everything that's happening. But the people here - they seem...happy."

"For the most part," Nina says, "we are happy."

"When my mother comes," Dara says, "you might have to reassess that."

I lie down on my bed and think about tomorrow. I realize that I have to do something. I can't let these people suffer because of my presence here.

As I lie on my bed roll a plan starts to form in my mind. Now I just need the courage to carry it out.

Chapter 20

I don't know what time it is when I wake up, but I push myself up onto my elbows and shake Nina awake, then Dara.

"We're going," I say. "Nina, go wake the boys."

Nina gets up, lights a lamp, and goes to the other room while Dara and I prepare ourselves.

"Did you sleep?" I ask.

"Some," Dara replies, but her eyes still seem hard and on edge. Dara scowls as she checks the corner of the room. "They've hidden my robes. Now I have to meet the queen looking like *this*." She gestures down to her Wildrian plant fiber clothes.

I don't know what to say, so I don't say anything. Instead, I join Aden and Naru in the common room. Soon, Nina and Dara meet us there as well, and the two Wildrian siblings lead us out to the dock, where we find a set of dark and hollow eyes looking up at us from the water. A pink light rises on the horizon, and in the air, I spot several birds that don't look quite right either.

"We're coming," Dara calls down to the eyes below the water. And then, out of a swirling mist on the horizon appears a huge ship with dark sails and the same elaborate woodwork as Spell Racer. It must be five to six times larger, though.

"The Sea Empress," Dara whispers.

"Come on," Nina says. "We'll take some canoes."

And then, unexpectedly, I hear a horn sound loudly into the quiet of the morning.

"The lookouts have raised the alarm!" Nina cries under her breath.

"Hurry," I say, "we have to get out there before a battle erupts."

"A battle?" a familiar voice says from behind me. "There won't be any battle. You trust me, right?"

"Sunny," I say, turning to look at the boy and his goofy smile.

"I'll help you get on your way," Sunny says as he hops down into one of the canoes. Dara pulls me into the other canoe, and Nina jumps in as well. When I look back at the Sea Empress, I find that a much smaller vessel – but one significantly larger than our canoes – is being lowered from the stern of the giant ship.

"The Hexeter," Dara says as soon as the boat sets off in our direction. Several ballistas are trained in our direction from the ship's main deck, where many dark-robed scarabs stand. My skin crawl as their faceless hoods stare in my direction and their chimeras circle in the skies above and in the waters below.

"Are you sure this is a good idea?" I call out to Sunny, who rides with the boys, as we begin to paddle.

"I thought you wanted to go to Witch Marsh," Sunny replies, "or have you changed your mind?"

I don't answer right away. "What if I have?" I ask.

"Then very good," Sunny says, "and yet, the consequences of past decisions are not so easy to escape, are they? And even now, you could decide to try to take refuge on the island. And there would be a battle, and only Sandor knows who would live or who would die. But if you go to Jezrella now, she will take you to the Pit, and that is where I will be." "Why would she take me there?" I ask.

Sunny, instead of addressing me, says, "Dara, why would your mother take *you* to the pit?"

"To hear the voice of Notso," Dara says. "But my mother does things in her own time. And she would never take Dara to the Pit now - not when you're here. She might take us to the Pit next year, or in twenty years. She'll want to spend time with Ayda before then."

"Why?" I ask. "Why does she want to spend time with me?"

"Your gift, Ayda," Sunny says. "The gift Sandor gives to every Centenary Sacrifice - True Sight."

"Wait," I say, "what does that mean?"

"That you have the ability to see things as they are," Sunny says. "It is a gift meant to help you make the right choice."

"To..." I pause, "sacrifice myself?"

"Yes," Sunny says. "But as Dara likely knows, Jezrella wishes to use your gift for her own ends - that is, before she makes you one of her children, before she makes you into one of the Condemned who she calls exalted and who only do the will of their master. She wishes to use that sight."

Even now I can see their dark, faceless hoods staring on at us from the Hexeter as the long oars push the vessel in our direction. I hear shouts from behind us as the Wildrians prepare for battle.

"Don't worry," Sunny calls from his canoe. "Jezrella will take you directly to the Pit. And that is where I will be."

"You seem awfully sure of yourself," Dara says.

"I am sure of my purpose," Sunny replies. "Ayda has made her choice. She has chosen to act, and so will I."

I don't look at either of them, though, because my eyes remain locked on the Hexeter as it approaches us. And there, between the mass of black hooded scarabs, I see the glint of jewelry. My heart quickens as the men rowing stop their exertions to throw a rope out to us. Nina ties it to the canoe's side, and soon the men are hauling us up next to the Hexeter and pulling us aboard.

Then the crowd of scarabs parts, and I see Jezrella for the first time, and she is the most beautiful girl I've ever seen. I am struck by her seeming youth; she appears almost younger than her own daughter. A diamond-encrusted crown of spikes tops her head, and slashing sashes of black with silver trimmings cover her body. And there on her chest rests a pendant with an icy blue jewel set in its middle. There's a certain severity to her beauty, like the lines of it are too sharp.

"Queen Jezrella," Dara says, kneeling with her face to the ground. "I am returned to you unharmed. And here is the Centernary, Ayda, her companions, and the Wilder."

"And are *you* one of her companions, *daughter?*" Jezrella asks. Instead of waiting for an answer, she turns and says, "And hello, Sunny. Still up to your schemes, I see."

"Hello, Shana," Sunny says. "Your end is near, and somehow you are even uglier than the last time I saw you."

Jezrella's nose crinkles, and for a moment I think I can see what Sunny is talking about, like she's a walking corpse dressed up in so much gaudy jewelry. But I only see it for a moment.

"So Ayda is the new one," Jezrella says, taking a few steps towards me with an appraising look from top to bottom. "I think she's maybe pluckier than the last? Some new clothes will help. Too bad Rollo had to go so quickly last time, but this one I have higher hopes for."

"But of course," Sunny says.

"And I suppose you want a free ride to Witch Marsh with the rest of them?" Jezrella asks.

"No, Shana," Sunny replies. "I will make my own way."

"Oh, what a treat!" Jezrella replies. "I'll have her all to myself. But this is too good to be true, isn't it? What do you have up your sleeve, Sunny? I usually can't get rid of you until your year is up."

"Just this," Sunny says, and with that, he steps forward, snatches the amulet from around Jezrella's neck, races to the railing of the Hexeter, and jumps over as Jezrella screams more shrilly than a scarab. The chimeras immediately give chase as her dark hooded enforcers scramble to the railing. There, I see Sunny racing along the top of the water, holding onto the dorsal fin of a dolphin as the chimeras fly and swim after him.

"Go," Jezrella screams to one of her scarabs, "bring the book!"

The scarabs rush about in their black robes and quickly bring a chest from the back of the boat. They unlock it and set it dutifully before Jezrella, who hastily pulls a book out and flips through its pages until she lands where she wants, pauses to go over things in her mind, stands up straight, and with great poise calls out, *"Let the winds rise up from the north to cover my ugliness. Let the waters rise up to cover my shame. Share."*

Something explodes out of Jezrella, and I watch as the oarsmen around me start falling to the deck, clutching themselves until they stop moving, and I can't tell if they are dead or just unconscious.

And there I see it moving on the waters - the white cap waves and dimpled water coming like so many swarming fish. And behind it, the water rises up higher and higher.

"Bring back that amulet!" Jezrella shrieks as the wave rises up over the ship.

"Uh, hey," Aden says.

"Hold onto something!" Nina interjects as she dives for the mast. I just manage to grab hold of Nina as the water slams over me, battering me wildly and almost breaking my hold on Nina's waist. When we roll back in the other direction and the water recedes, I struggle to push myself up and look around.

Nina, Naru, Dara - my breath catches. "Aden!" I cry. "He must be...he can't - *he can't swim!*"

With a flying leap, Naru jumps overboard. Several moments pass in terrifying suspense until Naru breaks the water, hauling Aden up along with him. Dara throws a rope, and they pull him up onto the deck and pump his chest until he coughs up seawater.

"You really need to learn how to swim," Nina says, almost scoldingly, while Aden still catches his breath.

"Will you teach me?" he asks.

But before I can hear Nina's answer, Jezrella's tirade eclipses my attention.

"You will find it! You will search and search and search until it is found! I don't care how long it takes. Every chimera - *go!*"

Then Jezrella's attention falls on us. I cower under her withering glare. "*You*," she says, pointing directly at me. "*You are part of this treachery!*"

"Mother, she didn't know," Dara cries. "None of us knew. Sunny didn't say anything about taking your amulet!"

"All he said," I say, "is that he would be in the Pit."

"The Pit," Jezrella says, giving a strange laugh as she says it. "He took my amulet to the Pit? I *must* have it back. Well, let's see then - I'll take you two," she says, pointing to Dara and me. "Kill the rest."

"*Or*," I say, "you could take *all* of us. I'm sure you want the best possible bargaining position. You're bargaining for your life, after all."

Jezrella pauses with a look in her eye that I can't place exactly, whether it's malevolence or admiration or some other unknown emotion in between. "Yes, *all* of you," she says, "That way, if he refuses, I can kill some of you to show him that I mean business. Now, hold on. We wouldn't want to lose one of you before I can get my amulet back, would we?"

The Hexeter lurches, and I just catch myself as the boat rises from the water. I stare up and find the cranes lifting it skyward with hooks on either side of the boat until our deck levels out with the deck of the Sea Empress. Then the gates open to allow us onto the much larger ship.

"So little time," Jezerella says. Then she turns to one of her scarabs and says, "Lock them in the brig and ensure that they speak to no one."

Soon, my hands are tied behind me, and a guard pushes a bag over my head.

"I'll see you soon," a voice whispers in my ear. I can't tell if Jezrella has just issued me an invitation or a threat.

Chapter 21

I had hoped we would all be put in a cage like the tributes on the Spell Racer, but when the bag is finally pulled from my head, I find myself looking at a long board nailed to a wall with several rings attached, and chains threaded through the holes of those rings that end in cuffs that are soon fitted on our wrists. So here we are, forced to sit in a line staring at a wall.

At first, we sit there dumbly adjusting to our new situation. Dara is on my left, Nina is on my right, Naru is after her, and Aden sits last at the end.

"Well, we're alive," Aden says finally. "And no one died. And Jezrella is taking us to the Pit. So Sunny was right."

"There's still plenty of time for my mother to kill us," Dara says.

"I guess the question then is whether we trust Sunny or not," Nina counters.

Dara shakes her head grimly. "My mother is right about him," Dara says. "He has schemes within schemes. Any miscalculation and we're all dead."

"Sunny," I say, but just as I'm about to come to his defense, someone pulls the cloth bag back over my head.

"*Jezrella will see you now, Centenary,*" a woman's voice says to me.

Hands pull the cuffs from my wrists. Then, when I struggle to rise, I am pulled up and dragged away.

Sunny, I hope you're out there somewhere, I think.

You do? Why don't you just open your eyes? a voice says somewhere in the recesses of my mind.

In the bag, my eyes are closed, but strangely enough, I become aware of globes like stars in the night sky at the center of people. And these globes have their own sort of light, even with the dark gloopiness mixed in, and from that light I can make out the outlines of forms surrounding them. And I see the woman pulling me along – older than me, worn down by a hard life but still alive. And behind her, there's another person they drag along, and somehow, just from the globe in her center, I can tell that it's Dara.

We're pushed down into two chairs. Our handlers stand ready, but, for the moment, we wait there in the dark.

"The queen tarries," the woman standing next to Dara whispers.

"She has been acting strangely ever since these prisoners were taken at Wildria," the other woman who stands above me replies.

"Shush," the other says. "Here she comes!"

Someone enters the chamber from the far side, but I can barely see her until the bag is pulled from my head, my eyes open, and I find the visible world overlaid on the lights I saw before. I stare at Jezrella, who is flanked by two of her scarabs. I could not see the scarabs at all with my eyes closed, so I try to look at them now, and I even close my eyes to try again, and my heart skips a beat as I make out their forms - not as lights but as even greater darknesses - much like the chimera I first saw on the riverbank. I try to turn my attention back to Jezrella's inner light when her voice catches me.

"Dara," Jezrella says. She extends her hand to her daughter. "Come, join me."

Tepidly, Dara stands, walks over to her mother's throne, and kneels at the dais. When Dara raises her head, her eyes lock on the amulet around her mother's neck. Having seen the first one only for a few moments before

Sunny snatched it, I might believe that it is authentic, but when I look with my other eye, I quite easily discover that it has no power whatsoever. It's just good enough to fool anyone who isn't looking for a fake.

"Now, Dara," Jezrella says, "your crew members tell me that you allowed the Centenary to beguile you. I can't help thinking that compromised loyalties led to the death of your sister, Mira, even if it was at the hands of Sunny, the Wilder."

"He is more dangerous than I expected, my queen," Dara says with shallow breaths, "but my decision to hunt Wilder captives had nothing to do with the Centenary. It was my own failing."

"Failure cannot go unpunished," Jezrella says icily. "Rachelle, show me a little conviction and do an agony hex on my daughter."

Rachelle, the woman beside me, immediately looks uneasy as she turns towards Dara, who stares down the older woman with grim determination.

"What Rachelle?" Jezrella asks. "Are you still a little soft on my daughter? Was watching her as a little girl so damaging to your resolve?"

"No, my queen," Rachelle says as the other woman fits Dara with a gag.

"Wait!" I exclaim, "What's the gag for?"

"Tana," Jezrella says, "please enlighten our Centenary."

The woman fitting the gag replies. "The gag does two things. One, it keeps those who are being punished from biting their tongues. More importantly, though, it keeps them from shifting their pain to one of their shifts."

"You see," Jezrella adds, "a witch's tongue is her most powerful weapon."

"If you are so powerful," I say, "then why don't *you* do the spell?"

"*Ayda*," Dara coughs through her gag as she shakes her head for me to stop.

"Oh," Jezrella says, "I *could*. Why not - *As wretchedness brings agony to my soul, so your body will writhe in agony!*"

And there inside Jezrella, I see a small fleck of light encircled by a mass of that foreign, gloopy matter. The gloop contracts right before it pops like a pustule burred with a speck of that golden light that glows gray through its capsule of goo as it shoots off to explode inside Dara's body.

I race over to Dara, who writhes with muffled grunts on the ground next to me. Those little shards of light burn away as the gloop seems to consume them, and with their passing, Dara finally stops thrashing and lies still.

"Have I passed your test?" Jezrella asks. "Am I powerful enough, or should I try again? *As wretchedness -*"

"I wouldn't do that if I were you," I say, almost before I can help myself.

"Oh," Jezrella asks, "and why not?"

"Your next spell," I say, looking at the shred of light still inside of her, "well, it may be your last."

Jezrella pauses, aghast. "Lies!" she cries.

"I'm telling the truth," I insist. "I've seen it. Your soul is nothing more than a speck. Without a soul, you'll, you'll..."

"Enough of this! Rachelle, take her away. I won't be goaded into killing you, *girl*. Not before I have my amulet back!" As soon as she's said the words, though, I can see that she's made an error.

Rachelle and Tana both halt and look back at their queen, scrutinizing the fake amulet on the queen's chest for only a single moment before they snap back to themselves and pull me and Dara back through the doors.

"Put the bag back on her head!" Tana calls." The bag crashes back over my head before Rachelle's nails dig into my flesh. Dark light pulses from within her. In another little bit, she pulls the hood back off and claps my wrists back into shackles, but I grab her sleeve and hold her.

"What are you planning?" I demand, but Rachelle pushes me off so hard that her hood falls off her head, revealing beautiful auburn hair streaked with silver that she quickly hides away. In another moment, she's gone.

Chapter 22

Words in the darkness wake me.

"Rachelle is dead," Tana says.

As I rub the sleep out of my eyes, I realize Tana is talking to Dara, not to me. In fact, the woman's true task is to deliver our midday meal of meat scraps and bread, which she hands to each of us.

"Thank you," I say. "And also for the news. How did she die?"

"Isn't it obvious?" Dara asks bitterly. "She made an attempt on the Queen's life."

"Wait – Really?" I ask.

"Of course," Tana replies. "Our queen has survived many attempts, and Rachelle...she was unhappy. That's all I can say. I have to return now."

Tana disappears.

We eat in a silence made heavy by the tragic news. It weighs on me.

"Did I..." I say, "Did I - did what I said earlier...about..."

"Did you get Rachelle killed by suggesting that my mother is vulnerable?" Dara finishes for me.

"Yes," I say with a gulp.

"You didn't *make* her do anything," Aden says from the other end of our line.

"It's strange how a little bit of hope makes people do crazy things," Dara says, "isn't it?"

"What does *that* mean?" I ask.

Dara remains silent, brooding for several moments before she says, "You're ready to do it, aren't you? You're ready to go and sacrifice yourself in the Pit."

I take a deep breath. Everything I've gone through in these past few days rolls through my mind. My time running from the ministry, living among witches for a voyage on the Spell Racer, and a brief time with the Wilders. And now - just now - Rachelle died trying to kill a woman she hated, a woman who had enslaved her. I could see in her all that hate and anger. But that's not what I feel. No - I'm actually thinking about Sunny.

"I think I am," I say at last.

Instead of dwelling on that thought, though, I ask, "Who was Rachelle? I don't feel like we know anything about her."

Dara grimaces and looks over to me. "She attended my mother for a long time - so long that the queen used to pass me off to her whenever my caretaker couldn't take me. For a while, I thought Rochelle cared about me, but she just wanted what everyone always wants in Witch Marsh – to get influence with my mother. She thought she could get it through me, but after a while, she stopped trying, and I wondered if she had just given up or if she realized that my mother won't ever want her for anything more than folding sheets. And now she's dead. And I wish I could say I'd never seen anything like this before, but I have. At least one person fails to kill my mother about every other year."

"Have they ever tried to kill you?" I ask.

Dara laughs bitterly. "No. I'm not that important. Everyone knows my mother doesn't care about me."

"*We* care," I say. Nina and Nara look at each other, and I hope that I speak for them as well.

After this, we settle into a quiet period until Aden starts talking past Naru with Nina about plant species she's encountered in her journeys to

Landria. It occurs to me that the two of them would get along remarkably well with Ma, and then the strange thought comes to me that perhaps Aden should have been the healer instead of me. And if that's true, what should I have been? A deacon? The question is rhetorical because there are no female deacons. Even still, the question remains - who is my father? I try to recall everything I know about Mr. Jeffries, a man I saw so many times coming to our hut for Ma's tincture. I remember his smiles, him asking me about what I was doing. For some time, I had a fondness for him before I learned to mistrust the cassocks.

"Ugh," Naru says. "This is so boring!"

"Be happy that things aren't more interesting," Nina replies. "They could be torturing us right now."

Naru just replies with a glare.

The wait drags on, and I start wondering when or if an evening meal will come, until I feel a strange tug inside of me. I turn my head, and Sunny has seated himself behind Dara and me, plain as ever.

"Well," Sunny says, "here we are, almost to the last leg of our journey."

"Wait. What are you doing here?" I cry. Then in a hushed voice I whisper, "*If Jezrella sees you here she'll...*"

Sunny smiles so widely that I immediately feel foolish.

"She'll negotiate for her amulet," Dara says. "She'll assume that you weren't stupid enough to bring it on the boat."

"You're right," Sunny says, "it's not here, and your concern for me, Ayda, is touching, but I don't expect Jezrella to find me or take me captive."

"You trust a lot in your expectations," Naru says from down the line. "Maybe I should expect to be freed from here. Would that help?"

"It would," Sunny says, producing a key from his pocket, which he tosses over to Naru, who slides it easily into the cuffs at his wrists.

"I present each of you with the option to leave here if you wish, including you, Ayda. Staying here is a sure path to the Crater's Pit. It is not an easy road, and death is a very real possibility."

"And escaping with you is less dangerous?" Naru asks.

"Ah," Sunny smiles. "Naru, you have a good point! Whether you stay or go, who is to say what might happen? Even still, if you would like to go, I will assist your escape."

All of my friends look from one to the other.

"I don't know," Nina says. "How did Naru and I even get caught up in all of this? We shared our dwelling with you and decided to go with you, but are we even needed anymore if Jezrella takes you to the Pit?"

"Everyone has a part to play," Sunny says, "but you're right. Maybe your part diverges from theirs. Maybe for you, to go is better than to stay."

"I think we should go," Naru says. "This has nothing to do with us."

"On the contrary," Sunny says, "it has everything to do with you – and everything to do with everyone. But that doesn't mean you should stay. It is better, I think, for you to consider your own part."

"I think we should also go," Nina says. "There's no reason all of us should be trapped by Jezrella."

"Ah," Sunny says. "Now *that* is a logical thought." Naru hands the key to Nina, who quickly unlocks herself.

"And what about me?" Dara asks.

"The path back is with the Wilder people," Sunny says. "They are Nina and Naru's people, but they are not *your* people. They will be going to the mountains. If you went with them, you wouldn't have to play any further role in this struggle. You could be free from your mother. You could sit out Ayda's confrontation with Notso. Whatever happens."

Dara pauses for a moment. "I'll stay," she says.

"Are you sure?" I ask. "You don't have to stay. You're mother tor-"

"I said I'll stay!" Dara shouts.

The ferocity of her response shocks me for a moment until I shake it off, nodding. "Right," I say. Then I look at Sunny and ask, "The amulet – have you hidden it?"

"No, and yes," Sunny replies.

"Do you ever stop talking in riddles?" Naru asks.

"No, and yes," Sunny replies, smiling even wider this time. "The stone that holds the word is hidden insofar as it went back to its owner as soon as I touched it."

"As soon as you touched it?" I ask.

"As soon as I touched it," Sunny replies.

"And that's *not* Jezrella?" Nina asks.

"No," Sunny says.

We all look at one another, but this seems so strange that we don't really know what to say.

"Just know that it *will* be in the Pit, and I *also* will be in the Pit, just like I said. Now, Aden, I suspect you're still in?" Sunny asks.

"Of course," Aden says with a simple smile. "But why don't we all just escape?"

"A good question," Sunny says. "At first glance, it seems like a wonderful idea. But let's investigate. We first have to ask, why did Ayda surrender herself to Jezrella to begin with?"

"So they wouldn't attack Wildria," I say.

"And at this moment," Sunny says, "what would Jezrella do if all of you disappeared?"

"If she couldn't get to me she might still race to the Pit to try to regain her amulet," I say.

"Yes," Sunny says.

"So?" I say. "Let's escape."

Sunny smiles, but his smile is thin and sad. "Yes," he says, "let's."

Nina passes me the key, and I unlock my cuffs. Then I pass it to Dara, and she unlocks hers. We all stand and look to Sunny for our next direction.

"This way," Sunny says.

"Wait," Aden says. "What do we do if…you know…if we run into someone?"

"Like that?" Sunny asks as a random crewmember turns the corner. "We keep walking." The crewmember passes by. "One of the things about witches," Sunny says, "is that they learn early on to keep everything to themselves. Standing out is a bad thing. While they may want promotions, they know that they're just as likely to have their accomplishments stolen by their superiors. No matter how many shifts they take or witches they convert, Witch Marsh will always be undercut by the fear of its least powerful members. The fear drives them forward, but it also holds them back."

"It didn't hold them back in our war with Zandria," Dara exclaims.

"You didn't quite *win*, though," Sunny says, "did you? And your mother has expunged all records of your most notable conflicts with the Wilders."

"What's going on?" I ask.

"We're here," Sunny says. "That stairway leads to the main deck. This is your last chance."

"Let's go," I say.

"Of course," Sunny replies. "After you. And remember - open your eyes. This was a good choice, even if it doesn't work out the way you think."

"What?"

Dara throws her arm around my neck, pulls me back, and I almost pass out from the pressure put on my wind pipe.

"Get back!" she cries. "Guards - the prisoners are escaping! Sound the alarm!"

"Over the side," Sunny directs the others, but he does not go himself. Instead, he approaches Dara where she's holding me by the neck.

"Get away," Dara says. "Get back!"

Sunny stands there, even as several hexes hit him without effect. "Do you trust me?" Sunny asks. I'm staring straight into his eyes. I try to nod.

"I'll see you in the Pit," he says just as the first crewmember reaches him. He turns, and the crewmate crashes to the deck. He sidesteps the next, dodges a sword, takes a running start, and dives with his arms extended as he flies over the railing to splash lightly into the water below.

"Dara!" I choke, but she tightens her grip on my neck until my eyes dim. Just before I go unconscious, I see the dark veins of the chimera's gloop running thick and sinuous into Dara's inner globe of light and for a moment I imagine that they're reaching out at me like tentacles ready to drown me in an inky sea of darkness.

Chapter 23

Darkness.

My eyes crack the tiniest bit open to a hazy room filled with candles, pink upholstery, and a flowery bed. My neck still hurts and I reach to touch it before I realize Dara sits next to me.

"Where am I?" I ask roughly.

"Rachelle's room," Dara replies before she takes a drink from a jug in her hand. "She was a sap. Look at all this stuff."

"Why?" I ask.

"Why this room?" Dara asks.

"No - *why did you do it?*"

"I'm her shift, Ayda," Dara says. "She can kill me any time she likes. And when I was out there in Wildria, I thought just maybe I could get away from her." Dara laughs.

"You *can* get away from her," I say.

"No. I was a fool. And you ensorceled me into being your friend," Dara says.

"I *am* your friend. And you're mine," I say.

"No," Dara says, shaking her head. "I have no friends." With that, she takes a long gulp from her jug. She smiles, and her eyes look glassy.

"What is that?" I ask.

"Oh, marsh-root tea?" Dara says. "You've never heard of it? I don't think the shifts on the plantations would survive without it. It dulls everything, just makes it all…all…right. I used to drink it a lot before I became a captain."

"Really," I say. "I didn't think you were this weak."

"*Weak?*" Dara says, spitting. "Let me tell you what's going to happen. We're going to take you to the Pit. My mother will get her amulet back. I'll be made like my brothers and sisters, and you'll die, and the world will go on for everyone else, but you'll be dead, one way or another, and I - I will be in Notso's world.""Notso's world?" I ask.

"Yes,' Dara says. "I've seen it. I've been to the Pit before, Ayda. I've met Notso. I visited Mira in that world - a world that she made for herself. Here, where we are, she was a shell of herself, controlled by Notso's servants, but in that place, she could do whatever she wanted, make anything she wanted, or experience anything she wanted. Jezrella took me every year to see her in the Pit, and I loved it. I loved them - and I'm not giving that up to be your friend."

"You're going to go live in a fantasy world and leave all the people here to their fate?" I ask.

"*Yes!*" Dara cries.

"You know, I thought I wanted to be a witch," I say, "but everything I've learned about them is everything I hate. They're selfish, power-hungry, cruel, manipulative cowards."

"Well, that's great," Dara says. "You can die thinking all those things, and then what?"

"And then…" I say, "and then…the power of witches will be broken."

"Not if I kill you right here and right now," Dara says.

"Well," I say. "What are you waiting for?"

Dara pauses. She looks at the jug in her hand, shakes with rage, and chucks it at the floor, where it explodes and spews the marsh-root tea everywhere. With that, she rushes out of the room and slams the door behind her, leaving me wrapped in the sweeping silence that follows.

It occurs to me as I stand here that she might be going to tell her mother right now about my desire to be the first Centenary Sacrifice to fulfill her obligation. Or that Sunny doesn't technically have her mother's amulet, whatever that meant when he told us. They might be coming to kill me right now. So I stare at the door and listen for footsteps.

Time passes by, and I eventually become bored and sit on the bed.

"What am I supposed to do now?" I ask aloud. "Sunny, how about it? Aren't you supposed to guide me? Where are you? Can Dara be saved?" I lie back and stare up at the ceiling. "Will it be worth it? Will I even be able to do it?"

I don't know what I expect as I lie here staring at the ceiling. Sunny isn't here. He doesn't answer. I try to remember everything he told me.

A few minutes later, my door opens, and something clatters to the floor. Dinner. But who left it?

Open your eyes.

I see the globe of light through the door and the outline of its bearer. I see Dara rushing away from me.

Chapter 24

Tana – not Dara – comes to collect me next.

"Where are you taking me?" I ask as she pulls me down the hallway, this time without the indignity of a bag over my head.

"The Queen will see you," Tana says, and almost as soon as she has said this, we enter the throne room where Jezrella sits with Dara on a seat one step lower and to her right, and behind her is a row of her other children, the scarabs, who are shadowed in black and look more like an absence than a presence.

I stare at Dara, who immediately looks away.

"Dara tells me that you are a true believer," Jezrella says. "I'm disappointed. You have the witch markings on your body, and yet somehow Sunny has twisted you in his direction instead of mine. Now, if I still had my amulet, you would be dead already. As it is, I may need you to bargain back for my amulet. I have survived another attack - the second in only a day's time. There are spies everywhere, so we must be on our way. In fact, I don't know who I can trust. So troubling..."

With that, Jezrella stabs herself in the abdomen and says, *Share.* Tana immediately falls to my right, clutching the blood stain that blossoms there. I fall down beside her and press the wound with her dress to stanch the blood.

"You can never be too careful," Jezrella says. "Come along. Take her"

The scarabs pull me off of Tana. "Keep holding the pressure on it!" I cry back at her as I'm dragged away. As long as she doesn't bleed out, she might be alright, but I'll never know what happens to her because I'm pulled up onto the deck where chaos reigns.

"Attack!" someone cries. A bolt of fire flies through the night sky and impales one of our masts, and that's when I see another ship tied to the Sea Emperess and its witch pirates boarding.

"Fight back or face my wrath!" Jezrella screams even as her scarabs hustle her and me to the back of the ship. As soon as we board the Hexeter, the last four scarabs man the twin capstans and begin to lower us down, not even stopping when one of them is set on fire. Their chimeras, meanwhile, wreak havoc on the attacking forces.

"Robare!" Jezrella screams. "I'll get you! I'll get you - you filthy skin-cutter!"

For the briefest moment, I see a man twirling a sword and wearing a bandage on the side of his neck. I gasp when I realize he must have cut Jezrella's mark completely from his body.

As soon as we hit the water, the masts are hurriedly raised, and the chimeras fly down with the scarabs who manned the capstans. We're racing off into the night with only the light of a waning moon for illumination. I look back and see the attacking ship cast off from the Sea Empress to give chase.

At first this chase seems slow to me, but I look around and every eye is trained squarely on our pursuers. "Will they catch us?" I ask over the roar of the sea.

"Really?" Dara asks. "You're wondering if they'll catch us? That's *Shadow Runner*, sister ship to Spell Runner. And the Hexeter is just my mother's dinghy to go traveling up rivers. *Yes, they're going to catch us.*"

I watch as they gain on the Hexeter. *Sunny*, I whisper, *I hope you knew what you were doing when -*

A huge fiery bolt flies off to the side of where I'm clutching the rail and sprays me in the face with its splash in the water.

"Get the book!" Jezrella cries, and there, from amongst the scarabs, emerges the locked chest. "Get a lantern. Dara, ready yourself for spellwork."

"No," I say, almost to myself. I shake my head. "No, this isn't right." I look out at the sea and the ship and the hexes that are racing our way. At such a distance, they seem weakened to fly so far, and yet one of them hits Dara, and she reaches for her eyes, suddenly unstable on the rolling sea.

"You, girl! Ayda," Jezrella shouts. "It will have to be you. Come here. I've written out the syllables. Say them with some hatred in your heart – or we'll all be dead!"

One of the scarabs holds a lantern over me as Jezrella places the scrap of paper in my hand. I look at it. *Let the tempest turn with fear as my worthless soul spins in isolation, and so hide us in the midst that binds our blinded souls.*

My lips quiver. "Sunny," I breathe.

"Do it!" Jezrella yells as she slaps me across the face - a slap that feels so familiar that I look to see if Miss Culbert could be on the other end of it.

"*Wind arise!*" I yell. "*Come to our aid as Sandor wills and save us from those who seek our harm!*" After the words of power have left me, I sag to my knees on the deck, but there is no searing pain in my body, and at first I worry that nothing has happened. When I look again, though, I see there above us a cloud turning, rotating, and lightning springing up from the sea.

"What have you done!" Jezrella screams, just as the twirling clouds reach down and touch the water like a finger. "Lower the masts and row! Row for broke, you filthy wraiths!"

The scarabs obey immediately as the winds rise and the twirling spout grows nearer and nearer. Shadow Racer, once in hot pursuit, now breaks off, seemingly intent on escaping the great funnel that rides upon the water, snaking this way and that. And there I see crew members jumping from the ship as the funnel meets it, sucking it in, tearing the mast off, and pulling it over. But then - as soon as the ship lies on its side - the column slows and begins to break apart. The lightning springing from it now ceases, and the great funnel disappears.

Jezrella glares at me in the lantern light but says nothing. Instead of answering her eyes, I kneel down next to Dara and try to comfort her in her blindness. The tracks of tears show on her face.

"It's alright," I say. "We're safe."

Dara shakes her head. "I'm a failure," she whispers to the ship deck.

"It's alright," I say again. "We're safe."

Dara doesn't listen to me, though. She keeps shaking her head and scowling, and I begin to wonder whether she's lost inside her head somehow. I try to think of what I might say with the words of power to help her, but nothing comes to my lips, so I hold her tight - something she tries to resist at first. We rock along with the sea, and I continue to repeat my words, "It's alright, we're safe," over and over again.

Chapter 25

I stay awake and watch over Dara as she sleeps.

It's not that I don't want to sleep, but it feels like something I need to do, and even when I get drowsy now and then, a look over at one of the scarabs or their chimeras is enough to wake me right back up again.

Eventually Dara starts to shift and finally sits up. She looks at me, and I smile.

"You can see," I say.

An uncertain look fills Dara's eyes as she remembers. "I'm not sure..." she says.

"We're safe," I say, cutting in. "It's alright."

Dara nods.

I look around the Hexeter and wonder if there's any breakfast. The scarabs row with their long oars because there's so little wind. And inside the canopy I find Jezrella sitting on her throne in the middle of the ship, her head slumped to one side and a streak of silver running through her hair. She no longer looks young. Instead, she seems to have aged twenty years or more in the time since the amulet was taken from her. When we approach her, she keeps her dejected glare focused somewhere far off in the distance.

"Everything's lost," the witch queen says. "All the Witch Lords will have turned skin-cutter by now. I feel myself losing more and more shifts. Someone must have sent a bird to Robare, and if he knows, birds will be flying all over Witch Marsh with the news. We will find no sanctuary, no path to my husband in the Pit."

"Your husband?" I ask.

"Notso," Jezrella says.

I look at Dara. "He's not my father," she says. "Actually, Robare's my father - not that he's spoken to me more than twice."

"You may want him to remember your connection when I die," Jezrella says, "because he may very well take the throne. All is lost – there's nothing for it."

Jezrella pulls a dagger from within her sleeves. "I suppose I will die knowing that I have killed my last Centenary sacrifice and kept that impudent Wilder from having his way one last time."

Then just as Jezrella steps forward to stab me, Dara cries, "Wait. There is a way."

"What? *What way?*" Jezrella demands as she stays her blade, letting it hang in the air as it waits to strike.

"We could go to the Zandrians' Miner's Camp on the other side of the Pit," Dara says. "I demanded that they bring their remaining tributes there. They won't know about your weakness."

Inspiration lights in Jezrella's eyes – but it disappears just as quickly. "There's no way we can get there. Witch Marsh lies between us and the camp. We could just as easily go straight to the Pit, climbing the Jaggar mountains."

"No," Dara says. "We'll fly. Mira - when she was trying to take Ayda to you - all of the stuff came out of her and made a huge bat. Look at all my brothers and sisters. Surely they can get us to the Miner's Camp. I can take the shifts. We'll go into the Pit and defeat all our enemies."

"And restore my throne," Jezrella says, eying her daughter.

"Of course," Dara replies.

"Well?" Jezrella says as she starts pulling the curtains of the canopy, rounding on the scarabs rowing us forward as well as those congregated at the back of the vessel. "You heard her – make us fly! Take us all the way to the Zandorians' mining camp!"

The scarabs, hidden in their dark hoods, look unmoved by the request until one of them steps forward and hisses, "*We will not be able to protect you, Majesty, if we do what you ask.*"

"We'll be flying, *fool*. I won't *need* you to protect me when all our enemies are on the ground!" Jezrella says.

The head scarab pauses there, perhaps thinking somewhere back in the dark recess of its hood before it answers, "As you wish."

Then the chimeras - many of which are flying in the sky, come fluttering down to their owners, who now space themselves around the Hexeter. The tar-like goop from within them then expands, consumes the chimeras, and comes together as a large bubble over the Hexeter, one that is tethered at the point where every scarab stands.

My legs buckle as we lurch and begin to rise.

How we maneuver, I have no idea, but the ship swings in a direction and I quickly spot the shoreline as we continue to gain altitude.

"Which Marsh," Dara says as we stand at the railing and gaze down on a green land with rivers and marshes stretching out before us. And as I see it, I can't help feeling conflicted inside. I wanted to reach this land for so long, and there it lies below me now, so close and yet out of reach. But as I see the settlements, I'm constantly reminded of why that dream died in me.

"What are those?" I ask, pointing.

"Rice fields," Dara says. Some of the laborers look up and point at us. A gigantic house stands in the middle of the plantation. Was this what I was coming here for - a life working a field or serving inside a large house?

We fly low enough that I can see the careworn expressions on the faces of the workers. The lights within them seem dimmed and eaten up by the dark goop.

"This is what you want?" I ask Dara, but she doesn't reply. Instead, she returns to her seat next to her mother's throne. She pulls her hair back into a bun and covers her head, though I wonder how well her hood will stay put in the wind up here.

Our journey has all the emotion of a funeral march, and I feel now more than ever like just a bargaining chip for Jezrella to get her amulet back. Did the night holding Dara on the deck of the rocking ship mean nothing?

I feel faint and stagger over to lean against one of the canopy's posts. – Am I just tired from staying up all night? Am I just hungry? Of is this what it feels like for Dara to choose her mother over me again?

Chapter 26

Hours pass. Eventually, I convince Jezrella to have the scarabs take us down into the trees to pick fruit to eat because we're all starving. I gather as many of these fruits – which Dara calls gawpas – into the Hexeter. They're sweet and fleshy with a grouping of seeds in a sort of case filled with jelly in the middle.

Once our journey resumes, we find ourselves floating among the Jaggar Mountains, which are a range of high rocky peaks that stretch through the whole middle of Landria. They're majestic, and sometimes we are above the clouds watching the peaks point up through them like a needle coming up through wool.

Besides the view, the ship offers little in the way of anything for me to do to pass the time. Dara won't speak to me, so I think back on everything that has happened since I was named the Centenary Sacrifice. The trip goes on and on, mountain after mountain, and soon the scenery even becomes dull to me.

Day becomes night, and I discover that any hope I had of seeing the Crater and the Pit from the air is dashed by the cloud cover and the dark. And even though I wonder whether the scarabs can still navigate without light, it doesn't seem like they even have mouths to communicate with now, so I keep my concern to myself, and nothing seems to come of it.

Waking in the morning, I prepare another breakfast of gawpas. Dara still sleeps at the back of the ship, and Jezrella barely nibbles on hers, sitting on the throne. She's become so gaunt now that I almost insist that she eat. Her face sags with wrinkles. Crow's feet step out from around her eyes. Her nose and ears look larger. Her hair has become a nest of gray and white. And when she finds me staring at her, she scowls.

"I'll become pretty again, and you'll still look like you," Jezrella says. "Then I'll stare at your dead body when we cast it aside and go on our merry way. Just you wait. It won't be long."

"You mean....we'll be there soon?" I ask.

"Before you try to serve me this rotting fruit again," Jezrella says, throwing her gawpas in my face.

I wipe my face, decide to ignore the Witch Queen's tantrum, and rush to the railing to search for signs that we're nearing the end of our trip. And then, I see it. A hole in the rocks here, carts of ore over there, and people - miners trekking through the mountains with pickaxes. It feels strange to see my own people again.

As we continue, I spot the camp in a valley. Most of the buildings are wooden structures, even though I see no trees around. Smoke billows from one large stone structure at the center of the camp. Carts of rocks pulled by mules go in and out its door. And there on the side of the camp is a familiar tent with Sandor's symbol - the staff and eagle atop it – the same tent I probably saw in Kern for the blossom festival, and I know for a certainty that in it we will find the Cassocks that we seek.

We don't descend into the mining camp directly, though. Instead, we pass it by. The rocky building with the smokestack sits on a stream, and the scarabs put the Hexeter down further on in its murky waters filled with the grit of the mining activities. Dara ties us up at a dock that I assume serves to bring supplies into the camp and takes metals and jewels away from it.

"*Now bring yourselves back together!*" Jezrella screams at her scarabs before jumping out onto the shore and hobbling along in the direction of the camp. She scowls, and Dara and I rush to catch up to her.

Up the path we pass a miner who looks like he's about to go into shock at the sight of us - either from Dara's robes and tattoos or my strangely weaved Wildrian clothes. Then we almost run straight into the Witch Queen's back when we round the corner of a building.

Jezrella turns to us with a severe face and says, "We mustn't let on that anything is out of place." Her scarabs catch up to us now. "We'll take our tributes and go," she continues. "And hopefully they'll be enough if we run into any minor skirmishes on the way into the Pit. And you," she says, grabbing me by the shoulder, "are not to speak."

With that, Jezrella gags me with a cloth while one of the scarabs binds my hands behind my back. Then I'm pushed along as we march up the stony pathway into the miner's camp and to the tent.

We're made to stop as the Zandrain Guards who were stationed at the doorway go in and consult with their masters before waving their gauntleted hands to bid us enter. When I'm pushed through the tent flap I catch my first glimpse of the children stationed at the side of the tent with a female attendant. The middle of the tent houses several Cassocks at desks writing in ledgers and reading accounts that appear small enough to have flown in by pigeon. Behind all of this, I find High Minister Fry himself scribbling away on papers. Then, when he looks up, his face appears devoid of emotion.

"We have come for what we are owed," Dara says, taking up the role of Witchland envoy once again.

"Of course," Fry says as he stands in his red vestments. "I am pleased to be done with this business," he says. Then he notices me. "*You*," he says, referring to me as he turns back to Dara. "Why isn't she dead yet?"

"She will die in our timing," Jezrella says, cutting in.

"And who are you?" Fry asks.

Dara shoots eyes at her mother. "She is...a member of our court," Dara replies. "The queen wishes to see Zandria's grave oversight in the matter of its tribute to be brought to a swift conclusion. Are these the tributes?"

Dara gestures to the children.

"They are," Fry says.

"Ayda!" someone shouts from the side of the tent, and there, unexpectedly, I see Ma rushing across the tent towards me. Two scarabs stand firmly in her way, and with my bindings, I am unable to say or do anything.

And then, to my even greater surprise, I see Mr. Jefferies come into the room with a crutch under his arm. It feels like forever ago that he fell off his horse as he hit me with a glancing blow that fateful morning.

"Ayda!" he calls, hobbling in. "Ayda!"

"Mr. Jeffries would like some information on the whereabouts of his son," Mr. Fry says. "He is unwilling to believe that his son could have willingly gone along with *this one*." He points to me.

A pained look comes over Mr. Jeffires's face. "I would like to know the whereabouts of my son," he says. "And as far as this sacrifice business goes, I think it's atrocious. It should be done away with. This girl should be returned to her mother!"

"*Deacon Jeffries!*" Mr. Fry says warningly. "*Remember your place.*"

"Let her speak!" Ma cries.

"No," Jezrella says flatly. "You will uphold your bargain, or you will know pain the likes of which you have never experienced before. The Centenary is ours, the tribute is ours, and now we will be on our way."

The scarabs go now to gather the children who are crying rather loudly, shrinking back from their new captors. I would like to tell Jezrella and Dara to leave them here, but I can't say anything. I wonder in this moment what

Sunny would do – Sunny, who never seems powerless at any moment. I try to look with my eyes, and I find my parents' light shining so amazingly brightly that I can't help but feel a certain sense of hope in it.

Then it occurs to me that the only way I can save these children is to run away so Jezrella will have to follow me instead of worrying about them. Fortunately, the cloth ties on my hands have loosened.

I give Ma and Mr. Jeffries one last look, throw my hand tie down on the ground, swipe the gag from my mouth, and sprint out of the tent with wild abandon.

Chapter 27

As I sprint across the rocky terrain, I consider the possible pitfall in my plan - if I don't outrun Jezrella and her forces long enough and for far enough, they will turn back around to reclaim the tributes. And they must follow me, because if I make it to the altar to sacrifice myself, then their magic will be gone.

When the first gloop hawk wings me, I go tumbling down a rocky hill, but I don't dare stay down for even a single moment. I jump up, quickly pat myself down, and let my fear drive me on. I dodge several more attempts by winged creatures to knock me off track. But then I see those failed assailants starting to merge into one another, and before long, my old enemy, the winged bat, closes in on me once again.

The clawed foot catches me by my shirt and picks me up until the garment tears, and I fall again to the ground. I scramble between some rocks then where the bat's feet can't reach, and I wonder for the first time whether this is a fight I can win.

And then, a sensation I've never felt before comes over me. I feel cold in a way I can't describe in places around my midsection and my thighs, and I realize in another moment that this chill comes from the site of every witch symbol tattooed on my body.

I feel the darkness in me wanting to merge with the greater darkness, and it's from these hooks that I'm dragged out from my hiding place and fall in front of the creature that has morphed into a form different from gloop bat – a form that I can't quite make out, but with a voice that sends shivers down my spine. *"Come to me."*

The dark form waits, and I feel my limbs moving. I stand up and walk against my will face-first into the tar-like darkness.

Sunny! I cry in my head, and in that pool of inky ice I feel the burgeoning of a strange warmth, but I can't quite grasp it, and strange visions swim in my mind – visions of Ma and Mr. Jeffries and Aden and Dara, but as the cold settles back on me again and the visions solidify, I cry out again, *Sunny!*

The dark sizzles as it peels itself off of me, screeching and hissing as my vision clears. I see straight through it even as the darkness flees from me. And for a moment, I think I see Sunny in the haze of the sunlight, but when I look, he isn't there.

The gloopy darkness forms back up into its bat form and launches itself into the sky, and, as I watch it fly away, I realize that it did not go in the direction I expected it to go – back towards Jezrella and Dara. Instead, it heads in the direction I am going – towards the Pit.

As the warm feeling dissipates, I continue onwards, now walking instead of running, which I don't have in me to do anymore. I hope I've put enough distance between the Witch Queen and me, but I've resigned myself now to whatever happens, trying to walk at a reasonable pace - but that is all I can do. I slowly, arduously make my way from one valley to the next, pressing onward in the direction of the Crater.

The memory of Ma in the Cassocks' tent rattles around my brain as I go, and also the man who must be my father and who – at the very least – made some sort of small attempt to save my life. And I feel strange that they don't understand what I intend to do, and how strange it is that, even as I have resigned myself to my own death, I feel more hope now than I've ever felt in my life. It seems a little unfortunate to me that I won't be able to explain this to them. But maybe, if I'm successful, they'll see the results and know. Maybe they'll come to understand after all.

Night comes, and I tuck myself into a crevice in the rock, trying my best to sleep in my uncomfortable condition and to go unnoticed by anyone trying to search for me. I don't think I will sleep until I'm suddenly awakened by blinding sunlight peeking over the mountain. So I get up and keep going - thirsty, hungry, sore.

I struggle on. Then, after some time, I begin to wonder if I'll ever find the Crater. The sun reaches its zenith, and I decide to take a break and pause in another crevice of rocks. I take the time to wonder if I will die from thirst, just fall over, and expire before I ever find the Crater or the Pit. I think perhaps I have done Jezrella's work for her.

And that's when I hear a sound.

Someone else. In fact, a few someones – are out walking up the incline very near to where I rest. I hug the rock that separates me from these people and try to peek around it to spy out who they might be, but I'm so wary of recapture that I don't allow myself to stick my head out too far.

And then I hear a familiar voice. "I can't believe Sunny let Chief Sorru send me home."

And another familiar male voice. "And I can't believe our uncle would keep us from the most important battle in our lifetime. It's not fair."

And lastly, a female voice. "Get over it. We've done plenty. Being held captive on Jezrella's ship is enough story to tell any one of our children or grandchildren."

I sit there in my hiding place a few moments longer with more happiness inside me than I could have ever thought possible. Then I pull myself up, walk out into the full light, and say, "Maybe your adventure isn't quite over just yet."

Chapter 28

Aden hugs me, which feels strange, but good, but the pressure of his arms reminds me that I was scuffed up in my escape. I wince.

"Get off her," Nina chides, shooing Aden away as she pulls the medical supplies from her pack, sits me down, and starts tending my scrapes. "Naru, hand her some water."

I drink deeply and wait as Nina dresses my scrapes and wounds with salve. Finally, she steps back and the three of my companions look at me. I put my hand out and Naru helps me to my feet.

"Are you still up for navigating for me, Naru?" I ask.

Naru nods.

"Nina?"

Nina smiles sadly as she bundles up the rags that are dirtied by my blood. "Of course," she says, stepping forward to give me a hug.

"Aden, your father is at the mining camp," I say. "If you want, you can go to him."

But Aden shakes his head. "No. I'm going to be right here by your side."

I nod. "Dara and the Queen are still out there. I escaped from them, but I'd prefer it if they didn't catch up with us."

"Well, you're in luck then," Naru says. "Evading enemy forces is my specialty." He takes a few moments to look up at the sun, survey our surroundings, and then sets us on our new course.

As we walk, I realize that I'm happy – happy to be among friends again. And I am happy for their support. And in every part and in every way that I am happy, I am also sad. I'm sad that I must leave them so soon, sad that it has taken all this time in my short life to find this place of contentment; I'm sad to lose it all. How strange it is to feel so happy and so sad at the same time.

And sadder still, the journey to the Crater is almost over before it begins. How could I have been so close and I never knew it? When we reach it, the mountains end as though they've been erased. I look out over the great expanse of the Crater and I can see straight across it in its entirety. It slopes down gradually, but if I had hoped for an empty path down to the Pit, I am disappointed to find the bowl is filled with what looks like black glass that has formed into spikes created by some explosive force that was frozen in place. Thousands of these spikes come up from the ground and grow outward from the center, ready to impale anyone who might accidentally fall on them.

"Wow," Aden says. "You've been in there?"

Naru shakes his head. "No, just seen it before. The Pit is supposed to be in the middle. Don't worry. *I* can find it."

"Can you find a way through these spikes?" I ask.

"Of course," Naru says, but I can see the concern on his face.

We circle around the edge for a little while before Naru finds a place that looks like we can fit through, and it's just in time because I think I can see other figures in the distance emerging out to the crater's edge.

"Here," Naru says, pointing to a break in the spikes where we are able to go in. We discover that the smaller spikes break easily under our feet, and we can break some of the larger ones by hitting them, but many are much too large for that, and we find ourselves in a maze of sorts.

"You wouldn't think it would be this hard," Aden says.

"No," I reply.

You didn't think it would be easy, did you?

We all stop.

"You heard that?" I ask.

"Vibrations from the crystal?" Nina asks, crouching to more carefully examine the dark glass.

"There is a substance," I say. "You have seen it - the one that makes up the chimeras. It is from the place where Notso is from, and I think it is embedded in these crystals."

Very perceptive. I control the crystals. They protect me from those who wish me harm. I hope you have not come to harm me or do anything so asinine as sacrificing yourself in the Pit. You think that it will work wonders, but trust me, your death would be a useless gesture.

"What do you mean?" I ask.

"What?" Nina asks as she stands and turns back to me.

"Didn't you hear what Notso just said?" I ask.

"That it won't be easy to get to the Pit," Naru replies.

I take a deep breath. "He was able to speak to me," I say. "Don't trust anything he says."

And then, just as I say this, several of the spikes become liquid and melt into the ground to create a smooth path forward, one that very quickly veers to the left. With very few other options, we uneasily start walking forward.

I now hold both you and your friends in my hand.

"Sunny won't let anything happen to us," I say, loud enough for all my friends to hear.

Like, he didn't let you get kidnapped by pirates? Or let Roland Hightower pick on you? Or let the good people of Kern look down on you? You came to me for help. You dressed yourself in my symbols - is it not so?

"I'm done with you and your symbols," I whisper.

Are you? I don't think you understand. I'm here to help you, Ayda. I'm here to give you everything you want. Has Sunny ever made such an offer?

"No," I whisper, "but he...he doesn't need to. He opened my eyes."

I can open your eyes in a very different way. Just relax, and I'll show you what life can be like with me. I know what you want, after all – you want to be a hero. You want to be accepted, loved, cherished. I can give you that. Can he?

"I don't want anything from you," I say.

Oh, really? How about this?

Chapter 29

All the crystal spikes suddenly disappear. I trip and find that I'm caught on a bed rather than stone or black glass. When I turn to push myself up, I discover that my clothes are different – they're no longer the Wildrian plant fibers but are instead a smooth, comfortable cloth that hugs my skin like a gentle embrace.

"Ayda, time to get up!" Ma calls somewhere in a hall beyond a room I now find myself in. But this is not Ma's hut back in Kern. There's no partition for privacy. Instead, I'm surrounded by stone walls. I'm resting on a cushy bed and find a painted vanity on the other side of the room. I rise in my nightgown and step into slippers placed conveniently where my feet land.

"Remember to spend some time doing your studies today!" Ma calls. Then she appears in my doorway wearing a green gown with a sash. Her hair is combed and washed, her face smooth and made up. I have always thought my mother was a beautiful woman, but I have never seen her like this. I never thought she cared much about dressing and beautification.

"Now, I don't want you to spend the whole day galivanting around with the guard," she says. "Why are you looking at me like that?"

"I... – what do you mean, 'galivanting around with the guard?'" I ask.

"You know," Mama says, "patrolling the highway, looking for trouble, hunting down brigands, and *avoiding* your studies." She pokes me in the ribs as she says this. "You know, your father may approve, but he was very serious about you interning at the embassy in Marshlandria."

"Interning in 'Marshlandria?'" I ask.

"Of course," Mama says. "Don't you remember? He talked with you about it last week."

"Ayda!" Aden calls from down the hall. "You promised you'd help me study for my exams for Monastery."

"Aden!" I cry. "What are you doing here?"

"What do you mean, what am I doing here?" he asks. "You know Da's renovating the library. And you know that I have to study."

"I...*guess*," I say. "What are you studying?"

"Theology, of course!" Ant replies. "Rodnas, help you - did you hit your head?"

"No," I say. "I don't think so. But who's Rodnas?"

"You know, Rodnas the creator," Ant says. "*Ma*, Ayda has another concussion!" he calls down the hall as a serving woman hurries by.

Ma comes quickly, takes me by the head, and starts looking for any contusions. "Did you fall off your horse?...Are you going to answer, or am I going to have to get an answer out of Roland?"

"Roland?" I ask with a gasp. "*ROLAND?*"

"You're right," Ma says. "He'll probably cover for you. Go see your father, though, before you go out again." Then she takes me aside to say privately, "Try not to let your brother down. Come back this afternoon. He likes to spend time with you, just here, not out there." Then, with a kiss on my forehead, Ma sweeps regally away down the hall after the serving woman.

"Aden," I call. "Where's...our father?"

"Da is in his study - come on," he calls, racing through our humongous home. I follow him and come to the study where Deacon Jeffries stands, poring over documents that look important. He looks up. "Oh, Ayda," he says, "you're not dressed."

I look down at my nightgown, suddenly ashamed of myself, but he just sighs and looks back down at his papers. I look over at the wall then and see a giant map of Landria. Zandria is where it should be, and Witch Marsh is suspiciously labeled Marshlandria, and the northern archipelago is just named 'Northern Archipelago.'

"The Wilders," I ask, "where are they? Where do they live?"

"What, Wilders, child?" the deacon asks. "What are *wilders*?"

"And the centenary sacrifice," I say, "is it the year of the centenary?"

"It's a year of jubilee," Aden says, "could that be what you mean? I'm excited for the festival."

"A sacrifice?" my father asks, "of what? Wherever did you get an idea like that? Is that something Roland came up with? I know you enjoy riding with the minister's boy, but sometimes I think we should get you some better company. Have you given any more thought about the Young Diplomats program I spoke with you about? I know you've always wanted to get out of here. Think of it – a chance to go to Marshlandria and meet some other budding young men and women from good families. What do you say?"

He looks like he cares – that's what I think. But it still feels incredibly foreign to me. "Where's Kat?" I ask.

"Your handmaiden?" Father asks. "I should wonder. Go see if she'll help you get ready for the day. And think about my proposal."

"I – I'll think about it," I say, rushing back through the hall. Kat's already in my room making my bed.

"Kat," I say.

"Katherine, my lady," she replies with a light bow.

"Kat," I say. "It's me."

"Of course, my lady," she says. "Here's your riding outfit. I had it cleaned from your fall yesterday. And Roland says his sister insisted on coming today."

"Evelyn?" I ask.

"Who's Evelyn?" Kat asks. "His sister's name is Dara."

"Dara?" I ask, but instead of waiting for an answer, I rush out of the room, down the stairs, out the door, and to the stables. I don't know how I know my way, but I do. The directions just seem to come to me like I've gone this way all my life.

And there, sitting astride two horses, are Dara and Roland. I'm struck by the appearance because I never imagined what Dara would look like without tattoos spiderwebbed across her face.

A stable boy leads a horse – *my* horse – out of the stables to meet me.

"Can you believe my older sister wanted to come out riding with us today?" Roland asks as though we should be friends instead of me and Dara.

"Of course," I reply as I mount up on Chestnut, which happens to be my horse's name. "In fact, she and I are about to leave you in our dust. Yah!"

We're off at a gallop, racing wildly through the fields, past the farm workers, the barns and silos, out into the woods until we rein our horses in to stop at the creek to let them drink. We've successfully lost Roland.

"That was fun," Dara says.

"It was," I say. "It was fun, and it's good to see you, but I know that none of this is real."

"Oh? And why shouldn't it be?" Dara asks as her horse drinks from the stream. "Isn't this what you wanted?"

"To be a Cassock?" I ask.

"Yes," Dara says, "to have the upbringing that your brother had, to have your family all together, to choose what you do from day to day, to help people. Isn't this everything you wanted? And if it's not, all you have to do is think it, and it will be real."

Sunny walks through the woods now, coming upon us very much like he did the first day I saw him. But I know that I have conjured him just by thinking of him, and that he's not real.

"You can *even* spend all the time you want with *him*," Dara says.

"I think I would like to speak to the real Sunny," I say.

"Who's to say that I'm not real?" Sunny asks.

"I do," I say, and just like that, Sunny fades away.

"I really wish you would be more willing to see what I want to do here," Dara says. "You're going to make things difficult for me – *and* for you."

"Let me guess," I say, "you can't kill me yourself, can you, *Notso?*"

Dara, who's actually Notso, smiles. Then he turns into a dark, glooping shape. There's nowhere to run when Notso chases me. The land starts disappearing before me. I trip in the blankness and try to escape, but I can't keep him from catching me. His icky gloop runs up my skin, starts encasing me, fills in every nook and cranny of my body until it runs down my screaming throat, and swallows me whole.

You're pretty perceptive, Ayda Cellars. But I'm resourceful.

"Right," I say, thankful to be free of the goop for the moment – now standing in a place where the darkness strangely glows like dying embers, "that's why you keep Jezrella around – to kill the centenary sacrifices before they get to the altar, isn't it?"

So perceptive, Ayda, but I'm perceptive too. You see, I know your secret – that one you don't want anyone else to know. In fact, if we tell those friends of yours exactly who you are and what you've done, they'll leave you here in your most desperate hour of need. They won't stick around to help someone like you to sacrifice yourself. And really, I should tell you that it won't work anyway. Your death can't buy back the words of power. They're mine, and you're mine.

"You're lying," I say, as I look around the great expanse of ember-burning darkness. And in it I perceive shadows – a great many of them. Chimeras without form. So many that I can't see the end of them.

My heart quickens.

"What is this place?" I ask.

This is my realm, Notso replies, *the realm of Abandon.*

"I would like to leave this place," I say as the shadows creep closer.

Really? We could go back and build whatever kind of reality you want to live in. Would that be preferable?

"I want my reality!" I scream.

Are you sure? Because, like I said, I know your secret. And what's more real than the truth about you? Should we go and tell your friends?

"You're bluffing," I say.

Oh, Ayda, you know I'm not. I was right there that day. I heard you whisper my words. I felt the murder in your heart. I'm the only one who understands you. I'm the only one who can love you. I'm the only one who can embrace your true nature. You're a murderer, like me.

Chapter 30

I'm suddenly back in the Crater with Nina, Naru, and Aden. The spikes have melted back down into the floor, and now it's just us in what looks like a humongous bowl of obsidian.

"You...you killed Roland," Aden says, breathily recovering from the vision Notso gave him.

"He's not dead!" I cry. "You told me that – you came to our hut and told me the morning when all of this started!"

"He died," Aden says. "If Sunny hadn't been there...You...you *killed* him."

"I was trying to protect my friend," I say. "I was trying to protect Kat! Roland was forcing her to eat a caterpillar."

"Some people eat those caterpillars," Aden says. "The woodsmen do. Where do you think Roland got the idea?"

"It was wrong," I say. "It was wrong, it was wrong - and I'm not sorry that I did it!"

The moment comes back to me now, running towards Kat as Roland holds the caterpillar above her, whispering the words – "*As my soul writhes in agony, as it fails in darkness, so your body will fail in weakness and your strength will be no more.*"

"I didn't think you were really a witch," Nina says. "And I know you hexed Naru and burned off his hair. I never thought...did - did you beguile us?" She starts to back away from me.

"Maybe this isn't such a great idea," Naru says, also backing away. "You're here. Do whatever you think you should. But I'm done."

"I think I am too," Nina says slowly.

Aden stays a moment longer and says, "Maybe you can still escape. You know, get as far away from here as possible and live on some remote island."

I don't move, but a tear rolls down my cheek. "What did he say to you?"

"He showed us," Aden says. "We heard the spell you cast when you were running at Roland. Your spell weakened his ribs so that when you hit them, they crunched. I was there – I remember it – and I can never unhear that sound. And now I've heard it again. I wish I'd never heard it, ever. He showed us Roland's death."

"He's a liar, Aden," I say.

"Not about this," he replies.

"You won't come with me?" I ask.

"I..." Aden says. "I..." Aden stops and grabs his head in his hands. "Did you really see Da at the Miner's Camp?"

"Yes," I say. "Is that where you'll go?"

"...no," Aden says. He shakes his head. "...I have a memory of my own – when Da came to me that morning. He said, 'She's your sister, Aden. We've got to go save her.' I didn't understand what he meant then, but I think I do now. I don't think I can save you. But I can be there, and that's something at least, I suppose."

I wrap Aden up in a big hug. He's stiff in my arms at first, but then he relaxes. "What now?" he asks when I let go.

I almost say something before I hear footsteps behind me. I turn around, hoping to find Nina and Naru returned to us, but instead I find Dara and an even more haggard and aged Jezrella.

"Are you here to kill me?" I ask Dara.

Dara's eyes are hard, but when she finally speaks, she says, "No, I'm only here to restore my mother and to set everything back in order."

"You'll die today, girl," Jezrella says, "but don't expect to make it to the altar." She grabs my shoulder violently and pulls me towards her, but Aden steps in, pushes her back, and struggles against her.

"Dara," Jezrella cries, "hex this boy!"

"Mother, stop this," Dara says instead. "We're all going to the same place. There's no need for this!"

"*No need?*" Jezrella cries before sharply slapping Dara across the face. "It's for power, you stupid girl! *There is always a need for power!*"

As Dara holds her face in the stinging aftermath of the slap, I step between her and her mother. "It must be terrible for you," I say, "to be so diminished. You don't *have* any power right now, and without it, you are nothing. It's all you had, and now it is gone."

Jezrella's face fills with rage. Her teeth clench, and her wrinkled cheeks contort, and in this moment, she has never looked more like the hags the ministry depicts witches to look like in their educational materials.

"*Oh, don't I?*" Jezrella asks. "Dara, *I* am the only one who can get what you want from Notso. You hex this sniveling light worshiper or I'll make sure you spend the next twenty years stomping mud in rice paddies as the lowest shift on Lord Silvin's plantation!"

Dara stands there for a moment. Then she whispers, "*As wretchedness brings agony to my soul, so your body will writhe in agony.*"

Aden falls to the ground convulsing, leaving Jezrella to reach her gnarled fingers in my direction and pull me roughly over to her with limbs that are surprisingly strong.

"Very good, daughter," Jezrella says. "Now, to get back my amulet. One hostage will have to do it." With that, she pulls a dagger from her sleeve and readies it to strike Aden, who still lies prone and helpless on the ground.

I – however – grab Jezrella's wrist, but she twists around on me, shoving me down, trying to shake free her deadly hand, but I don't let go, and soon she's falling down with me instead. She keeps struggling, but with a great scream, I push her hand and the blade into her chest just above her heart.

"As wretchedness brings agony to my soul, so your body will writhe in agony!" she cries. The words leave her mouth reflexively. And that last little shard of light inside her launches in my direction. Even as the burning tar-like substance explodes in my body, sending me into painful convulsions, I see Jezrella's eyes darken. She screams as the goop in her center grows and spreads outward, turning her into a scarab. She fights against it hopelessly. Her head falls to her chest, and when it rises again, I know that she is gone and that someone else remains.

In another moment, the spasms in my muscles from Jezrella's last vengeful act finally get the best of me, and I fall helplessly on my face to the rough glass floor of the crater.

Good Ayda, good! Come to me, my daughter. Come to me. We will let violence flow through you like an undammed river. Feel it rise in your blood. It is you who will succeed where Jezrella failed. You will slay the wicked. The oppressors will quake at your feet and be dismayed!

Chapter 31

I feel shaken. Even when the tremors in my body stop, I wait to get up.

When Aden finally helps me to my feet, I find that the new scarab has disappeared, and only Dara stands there waiting to confront me.

"You killed her," Dara says.

"No, I stabbed her," I say. "I think she actually killed herself...by accident. She was going to kill Aden. And she said the spell. And she died."

"You killed the Queen," Dara says again. And only now do I realize that there's no condemnation in her voice. "Do you know what that means? Now you have a claim to the throne of Witch Marsh."

"I don't *want* the throne of Witch Marsh," I say.

"I'll help you rule," Dara says. "I know these people. I've known them all my life. You've done the impossible – you killed the immortal Witch Queen. All you have to do is take my mother's amulet and Notso's blessing, and you'll have it all. No one will be able to stop you."

"Ayda will never accept," Aden says. "Never!"

They both look to me for an answer, but all I say is, "Come on. Let's get to the Pit."

The crater stretches out before us, and even though our side of the bowl has become smooth, the other side is still filled with jagged spikes, and as we near the Pit, we begin to hear shouting – war cries, cries of anguish, clashes and struggle, a great battle.

"Do you hear that?" I ask.

"Yes," a familiar voice says from behind me. "It's the sound of the Wilders holding back the Witch forces."

"Sunny!" I say, running to him for a hug before pulling back to see his goofy grin.

"You made it, Ayda," he says.

"She did," Dara says, stepping in, "and no thanks to *you*."

"It's not the time to debate what part I played in helping Ayda get here," Sunny says. "I'm here for Ayda. You have seen what Notso has done to this world. You have seen what will happen if he strengthens his grip. Unfortunately, you can't know what things were like before he came. The question is – are you ready to sacrifice yourself, your life, and your will – to help make things right? *And*, more importantly, do you trust me?" Sunny holds out his hand.

"*Ayda* will be the new queen of Witch Marsh!" Dara cries before I can answer.

"She won't," Aden cries back. "I don't care what that glob of tar says, I don't want my sister to ever turn into what we just saw!"

Aden lowers his voice and says, "Remember, Ayda, you can still walk away. We can still get you out of here."

"For how long?" I ask. I shake my head. "I have to make a choice, Aden. And I think I've made it. If my life can mean anything, I think it would be better if Landria were a bit more like Wildria."

I take Sunny's hand, and he pulls me into a hug. "I've done some things," I whisper into the bushiness of his hair. He pulls back, holds me by the shoulders, and says, "I know."

"And you still want me to do this?" I ask.

He smiles again. "Do you remember the part about trusting me?"

I nod.

"Good," Sunny says. "That's a very important part."

"I wish Naru and Nina had stayed," I say.

"They brought Aden to you," Sunny says. "And for now, that will be enough. But remember, not everyone will understand your purpose, nor will they look past your mistakes, but as long as you do what is right, Sandor will bless you."

I take a deep breath and nod as I step back, but when I do, I see Dara running in the direction of the Pit ahead of us.

"Should we be worried about that?" Aden asks, pointing.

"No," Sunny replies, "never worry. *But*...it *is* true that Dara will make things more difficult for us. Unfortunately, she is still deeply under Notso's sway."

"Wait – isn't there any hope for her?" I ask.

"There's always hope," Sunny says. "And there will be even more hope when we take back the words. Come on. It's time."

"Yes...time," I say to myself as we go.

The walk itself isn't very long, and once we get to the edge of this bowl-within-a-bowl that goes further down into the earth, the strange sight of the Pit fills our eyes. It appears verdant with grass, small shrubs, and a single bush in the center of it where Dara now stands. Off to one side is a pile of stones, and around that pile of stones, there appears to sleep the serpentine body of a dragon. At the far edge of the Pit, I see the battle between the Wildrians and the Witchlanders where it spills over. Darts and hexes fly, and some combatants accidentally stumble into the Pit and find themselves suddenly on grass rather than lifeless obsidian. After a second, they throw themselves back into the fray.

But then a man appears at the opposite side, graying and getting on in middle age, flanked on either side by several witches. He carries himself with an air of command, even though he and his comrades appear to have bandages on their necks.

"Father!" Dara calls.

"Let's approach," Sunny says, taking the first step onto the grass. Aden and I follow him down to the center, where Dara waits by the central bush. Robare and his lieutenants approach from the opposite side.

After a few moments of staring at one another, Robare asks his daughter, "Where is the Queen?"

"I have killed my mother, Jezrella, Queen of Witch Marsh," Dara announces. "And I hereby assert my claim to my mother's throne."

Not to be outdone, Robare immediately announces, "I, too, assert my claim to the throne as the most powerful Witch Lord in Witch Marsh."

Then, unexpectedly, the Pit quakes from a deep-throated growl that explodes like thunder. The dragon has awakened, pulling its serpentine body from the pile of rocks. It speaks.

"Behold, I am the Great Wyrm. Bow before me, you claimants of the Witchland throne."

Chapter 32

As Dara and her father turn to bow to the dragon, I whisper over to Sunny, "What are we supposed to do?"

"Notso is blocking us from the Altar," he says, pointing over to the pile of rocks.

"And I have to die on the Altar?" I ask. "Right here isn't close enough?"

"It must be on the altar," Sunny says.

Our side discussion is cut off by Notso's booming voice. "*Killing Jezrella is not enough to assure a claim to rule,*" he says. "*The one of you who kills the Centenary Sacrifice – that one will be crowned ruler of Witch Marsh and will be given Jezrella's spellbook and the amulet of eternal life.*"

Sunny steps in between the witches and me.

"*You have no power here, you wandering vagrant!*" Notso cries. "*Be gone!*"

"I do not need to have power here to stand in this place in the Centenary year," Sunny says. "And stand I will."

The dragon, incensed by Sunny's answers, bellows in rage, rears back, and appears ready to blow flames with white-hot intensity, when – instead – the dragon bursts apart into so many scarabs and chimeras who flock towards us like so many gloopy crows.

"They have no power to hurt you," Sunny says as he grabs me by the arm and hurries me towards a boulder with Aden rushing close behind. "But they can take you to those who would hurt you – Dara, Robare, or his servants."

Destroy them! Notso roars, seemingly still able to project his voice even though his dragon body flurries around me as so many bats, ravens, scarabs, and snakes. "*A crown to the first to kill the girl!*" it cries.

Sunny twirls deftly through the air, and any of the dark creatures he touches are immediately caught on fire and burned through to cinder. Even still, one of the crows scratches my cheek as it wings past me.

Several of the chimera bond together to form a gigantic, winged cat-beast that lithely circles around me, trying to get past Sunny's defense. I take refuge behind a boulder and almost collide with Dara as she spars with her father, running as he shoots hexes at her. Robare's servants, on the other hand, are stationed at the altar, ensuring that we don't get around him and make the sacrifice before he can confront me.

"What are we going to do!?" I cry at Sunny as the beast cat circles so close as to make a swipe for me, prompting me to break from the boulder to scramble towards the bush in the middle of the Pit.

"True Sight," Sunny says. "And when you need help, look to those who are close to you. And remember, Notso cannot be hurt by those of this realm, but he *can* be subdued by them." If Sunny intends to say any more than that, he is cut off by the winged cat who charges around him and lunges for me.

I scream and roll out of the way as the cat hits the bush instead and goes crashing away on the other side of it. It's wipeout trips Dara, whose knife throw hits her father in the chest, but not the heart. He pulls the dagger out, says the word *share*, and lets one of his lieutenants on the altar fall over instead as he charges towards his daughter, who scrambles to rise from the ground.

Sunny heads off the cat while I race towards my friend.

Just as Robare brings the dagger down to stab Dara in the chest, I tackle him, breaking the weapon from his grip as we go rolling through the grass. When we stop, Robare realizes his opportunity, puts his hands around my throat, and begins to squeeze.

I feel pretty stupid now as my vision blurs – but then it shifts, and I'm looking at Robare's globe and its dim light infested by veins of rot and ruin. The darkness of the cat beast contrasts wildly with Sunny's light, and then it occurs to me in this precarious moment near death to look for the darkest darkness. And there it is, strangely in the middle of the Pit. I might not have seen it if not for Aden's own light so close to it.

In the next moment I gasp and suck in a huge breath air and massage my neck, suddenly back looking at the visible world. "Aden!" I cry. "Find Notso. He's right there - in the middle of the Pit!"

Dara looks down on me, dagger in hand, her father lying nearby, unmoving.

"Are you going to kill me?" I cough, trying to regain my breath.

"I have to," Dara says with trembling hands.

"You don't have to be your mother," I say. "You don't have to be like your brothers and sisters. And you don't have to be like your father." I cast a glance over towards the altar and find that both of Robare's lieutenants - the ones who were still alive - have fled.

"You saved me," I say.

"Just for you to still die?" Dara asks. "Why shouldn't I get something from your death? Why shouldn't I rule Witch Marsh?"

"You will get something from it," I say, "but not what Notso wants to give you."

"I can't do it," Dara says, shaking her head, lowering the dagger closer and closer to my heart. "I'm sorry."

The tip of the blade pierces my skin, but just before it can go any further, Sunny gives a gigantic battle cry, grabs the cat beast by the tail, and hurls it at Dara. It explodes in flaming darkness before it reaches her, but the force of it knocks her back.

I scramble over to my friend. I check for her breath, then grab her wrist and feel the beating of her heart. Even though her eyes remain closed, I relax.

"You've done it," Notso says as I rise with the dagger in hand. *"You defeated your enemies like I knew you could. You have proven yourself worthy to take the throne. It's time to leave that silly boy behind and embrace your destiny. You are the true heir to Jezrella's throne. You have the right to power and glory. With me at your side, the Zandorians will grovel at your feet. They will rue the day that they made you feel unworthy. They will beg your forgiveness as you lay on them the heavy burdens they deserve and assign them their place among the shifts."*

"I think I found him!" Aden cries as I walk over to him.

I turn to Sunny, but he says, "I am not allowed to reveal his location to you. But why don't you go see what your brother has to say?" He grins.

"Look at this caterpillar," Aden says, holding up a branch from the bush.

"You're mistaken," the voice of Notso says haughtily. *"Do you think someone as great as I would be a caterpillar?"*

"Look at it," Aden says. "When Roland first talked about having Kat eat a caterpillar, I studied them extensively, and there's no caterpillar or grub in all of Landria that looks like this."

I look closely at the bug, and to my surprise, I see a miniature version of Jezrella's amulet around its neck. Furthermore, several similar stones appear along its back. "The great wyrm," I say, fully appreciating the irony. "How do we subdue him?"

"Maybe we can tie him up in this cloth napkin," Aden says, pulling one from his pocket.

"*No!*" Notso says. "*Don't waste your time with that caterpillar. You had better watch out. More shades are coming to attack you!*"

The dark remnants of the beast cat, somehow unburned, now congeal together even as Notso speaks, but just as Aden ties the cloth around the caterpillar, the tar-like gloop begins to lose its form and disappear altogether.

"Very good, Aden," Sunny says. "But now it is time."

Chapter 33

Time to die.

I turn to look at the altar. Here it is, the moment I tried so hard to escape and then so hard to embrace. It's now here, and I have no idea if I'm ready. Everything Minister Hightower said in his services about existence after death comes back to me now, everything I've done, including to Roland and Jezrella, all the cutting remarks to Ma, not getting to see Kat one more time, not appreciating my brother until just now.

"You can do it," Sunny says. "Do you trust me?"

"Yes," I say.

"Take my hand," Sunny says as he walks me towards the pile of rocks. It's a short walk and an even shorter climb to the top of the little rock pile.

"Lay yourself down," Sunny says. With a few deep breaths, I lay down on the top of the altar. It's uncomfortable, but I suppose I couldn't expect a bunch of rocks to feel like a straw mattress. Then, to my surprise, I hear footsteps, and Sorru, Nina, Naru, and several other Wildrians circle around.

"Friends," Sunny says, addressing those gathered. "This day is a day of great victory, but its greatest victory will now make your hearts sad for a time. Remember, though, what you have gained and go forward with courage to the calling that Sandor puts upon you. Ayda, when you're ready."

I take the dagger and find the spot where Dara pricked me over the heart. "Not there," Sunny says. "Here." He points to my abdomen.

"Are you sure?" I ask, realizing that my death will be much longer and more painful if I stab myself there.

"Yes, Ayda," Sunny says. "It must be there."

"I...I don't think I can do it," I say as the dagger shakes in my hand.

"Let me help you," Sorru says, tenderly putting his hands on mine. I close my eyes tightly, but tears still manage to stream down the sides of my face. It takes everything inside of me not to jump up off the altar and try to escape. The blade slips into my middle in one swift stroke, and the pain of it shoots through me.

Tears flow freely from those around me. Aden's face contorts in sorrowful agony as Sorru pulls out the dagger, and I gasp sharply. The blood flows from my wound, but I can't help wondering how long it will take to die, wishing every moment for an end to my suffering.

"Thank you, Ayda," Sunny says as he stands over me. "You have come to trust me, and now it is time to reward your trust and to bring an end to your suffering. Give me your hand."

With great difficulty, I raise my hand, and Sunny takes it. In that moment – when I hold his hand – a sense of peace comes over me. The tremors of pain racking through my body cease, and I stare up at him.

"One of Notso's most abominable perversions," Sunny says, "is what he did with the word *shift*." Sunny smiles as a single tear rolls down his face.

A feeling of wholeness and wellness suddenly comes over me, so much so that I sit up and look on in horror at the blood soaking Sunny's abdomen.

"Help put me into place," Sunny says weakly.

"But you can't die," Aden cries.

"No, Aden," Sunny says. "You misunderstand. No witch can kill me. But I was always the sacrifice. It was always going to be me. Ayda trusted me with her life, and now I give mine in her place. My life is the price for the return of the words, and it always was."

I'm healed. My wound is completely gone. I stand up uncertainly as though my legs might give out under my weight at any moment, and I catch myself on Naru, who helps to steady me. I don't know what to feel at this moment – elation that I have escaped death or a sorrow so great that it might as well kill me anyway, as I watch Sunny suffer. His blood leaks out all over the rocks of the altar, and he gasps for breath.

"We need you still," I say, kneeling down next to Sunny. "You can't go."

"I'm always nearer than you think," Sunny whispers with a smile.

"But what are we going to do?" I ask.

"Walk with me," Sunny whispers before he closes his eyes one last time. Sunny's dead.

I look between Aden, Nina, Naru, Sorru, and the others. What should be done? Should we pick him up? Bury him? But just as I reach down to touch him, Sunny's body emits a flash of brilliant light and is gone, leaving only his blood sprinkled over the rocks of the altar.

I'm suddenly overcome by the totality of his loss – the loss of his goofy smile, his poofy hair, his certainty, and his connection to the natural world. All gone. All lost. I cry out in rage at my grief. Doubts flood in – I hardly knew him. Why should I care? But I do care.

When I'm finally able to wipe my face, I look back down to the grass where Dara lies. She's still unconscious.

Chief Sorru pulls my attention back to him, though, and helps me to my feet. Holding my arm, he leads me down to the side of the altar and sits me on the grass. The rest follow and soon we are all sitting in the grass together.

"Today is a day of great deeds," Sorru says. "Today is a day we will remember for years and years to come. We will remember the sacrifice made this day to overcome the wyrm and his many deceits. Sunny who has always shown light in the darkest times has gone out from us. And Ayda, the last Centenary, has passed from death into life. And we will feast tonight. We celebrate tonight. But for now, let us renew our strength from a battle dearly fought.

I watch then as Wildrians begin taking meat and bread, nuts and fruits, out of pouches in their clothes and armor. As tears still flow down my cheeks I eat. And that's when I find Naru and Nina sitting down next to me.

Chapter 34

"We're sorry," Nina says.

I look at them.

"There didn't feel like there was time to say it before," Nina continues, "but we're sorry we left you."

I nod. "Right before he went, I told him," I say. "I told him what I'd done, and he said, 'I know.' And that was all. So I guess that's it. I know...I *know*."

Naru still hasn't said anything. His hard eyes look at me and I look back. "I know, Naru," I say, and he buries his head in his hands, but I pull him into an embrace, and we stay that way for a few minutes until I let go.

"You're alive," Naru says. "You're here."

I nod, pull up my shirt and look down at the scar on my stomach, left there I suppose to remind me of this day. I take another bite of the food that's piled in front of me. *From death to life*, I think.

Aden comes over now. Somehow he's been caught up in the celebration. Someone's painted his face and put hard bark greaves on his forearms.

"Ayda," Aden says, "I can't believe it."

"I know," I say. "I don't believe it either. I'm alive."

"I know," he says. "What does this even mean? What do we even do?"

"I don't know," I say. "What else is there to do? I was so worried about dying, I've hardly thought about living."

"You could come with us to Wildria," Nina offers.

I nod, but my thoughts are far away. The sun shines down on us but I feel like I'm lost in darkness. Is it because Sunny's gone? Will anything ever feel right again? And that's when look down to Aden's belt where he has a napkin tied – but there's a whole in it.

"Aden, look," I cry pointing. I grab the napkin off his belt and fling it open.

"He's gone!" I cry, rising to my feet. "He's gone! Everyone get up. Get up! Notso's escaped!"

I stumble around through the crowd looking wildly about in the grass and in the food. The warriors are startled by my erratic behavior and start standing as well. Aden starts calling for them to rise and search for the caterpillar. And that's when I look over and see Dara sit up from where she had been knocked unconscious – and on her chin I spy a dark furry line.

"He's here!" I cry. Everyone looks over to me as I leap to Dara's side – but I'm too late. The caterpillar has somehow made it past her teeth and down her throat. She pulls away from me when I reach her and says, "Hello, Ayda. I'm finally free."

Chapter 35

"D ara?" I ask.

"Oh, she's in here, but I don't think we'll see her for a while. A long, long while."

"Notso," I say. "Get out of her."

A Wildrian sleeping dart hits Dara in the chest, but Notso just smiles. "Silly, silly Wildrians," he says, shaking her head. "What do you know? Your friend will be queen of Witch Marsh after all."

"Your power is broken," I cry. "Give her back to me!"

"I think I like it inside here," Notso says. "And as for my power," – he grabs me under the arm and throws me several feet through the air - "it's looking good! Maybe I should have let Sandor kill himself ages ago."

"Sunny," I whisper, trying to rise, "help."

My vision blurs. Suddenly, I'm pulled to my feet, and the Pit looks very different from the way it did. It looks like charred waste. I just am able to see the backs of two people fleeing its rim, leaving two others standing there.

"Sunny!" I cry, but Sunny doesn't turn to look at me. He looks instead at the figure of a man made entirely of chimera gloop, holding several gems. "I have them," the figure says. "They're mine."

"They are, aren't they?" Sunny says. "You told them what I said was not so, and that is what I will call you here."

"Notso," the dark figure says, "it has quite a ring. I suppose I'll be going now. I'll need to catch up to those two. I have so much to teach them. Don't worry. I'll take care of them like they're my very own."

"Not so fast," Sunny says. "With the words you have stolen – my words – I bind you. This is where you will stay."

The gems that Notso holds suddenly attach themselves to his gloopy form, hissing and causing him to buckle and fall to the charred ground. His body shrivels and shrivels until it is nothing more than a little line of gloop studded with tiny little stones.

"I will not allow you to peddle your falsehoods so easily," Sunny says. "You will stay here."

"*They will come back to me,*" Notso says in a voice that seems to emanate from the air.

"Yes," Sunny replies. "They will."

"*You have accomplished nothing!*" Notso cries.

"We'll see what I accomplish," Sunny replies.

"*You want the words back,*" Notso says, "*and I wish to be free. Let's make a wager.*"

"What is your wager?" Sunny asks. "For what price would you give back the words I gave to my children?"

"*Your life and my freedom,*" Notso says, "*in exchange for the words.*"

"It is a high price," Sunny says, "but I will pay it."

"*Not so fast,*" Notso says. "*I have just gotten these words. I think I want to play with them first.*"

"For how long?" Sunny asks.

"*Let's say a hundred years,*" Notso says.

"And then I will pay for their return?" Sunny asks.

"*No,*" Notso says. "*No, no, no - they're mine!*"

"Then you don't wish to make a wager?" Sunny asks.

"No, I will," Notso says. *"But I think you should suffer a bit more. I feel the power of these words, and I don't want to give them up so quickly. Before you are able to pay the price, you must convince one of your children to walk with you, even to the point of giving up their own life on that pile of stones over there. And you can't tell them who you are. And if you fail for any reason, you will have to wait until the next hundredth year."*

"That is a very high price," Sunny says.

"But the only one I will accept," Notso says.

"In that case," Sunny says, "I must insist that the current rules governing this world will continue. Beings from our two realms may not interfere directly in this place without the consent of my children who live here. Their power of free will, I will not sacrifice."

"Is that a challenge?" Notso replies, *"I will show you how many I will corrupt. I will bring all of my creatures here. This realm will belong completely to me. Your children will become my children, and I will make of them what I wish. We will turn them into our vessels. We will oppress them and make them like us."*

A tear rolls down Sunny's face. "I know what you will do," he says. "The wager is struck."

"So it is," Notso replies. *"Now be gone! I have new toys to play with. I might even be able to get off one of these stones."*

Before Sunny turns to go, he says, "When the time comes, your schemes will fail."

"I have all the power here," Notso cries. *"The words are mine. And I win even when I lose!"*

"You are mistaken," Sunny replies.

Then Sunny looks at me. "When you fail," he says, still speaking to Notso, "you will be cast out by those who were chosen, by those who choose to walk with me, and by the very words you schemed to steal."

My vision blurs again, and I'm back in the present. I sit up in the grassy pit and look at my friend possessed by Notso.

"Ayda!" Aden cries as he rushes to my side from the altar. "What are we going to do?" he asks, crouched down beside me.

"The words," I say. "Give them to me."

Chapter 36

"You will give me back my friend," I say as I stand up with the word gems in my hands, which inexplicably melt into me.

Oh no – I'm afraid I've lost them! But as I stand there staring at my hands, I feel them inside of me. And they feel...*right*. I haven't lost Sunny completely, I think. These words, his words, are here with me.

I walk towards Notso, even as Aden calls out after me to stop.

"Should we see if I can kill you now that Sandor's gone?" Notso asks, taking Dara's witch robe and shedding it as he walks to meet me.

"I'm not afraid of you," I say.

"*We'll see about that*," Notso says as he throws a punch. I catch the fist in my hand, though, and Notso shrieks. He begins to shake uncontrollably, and just as suddenly, he stops.

"Dara?" I ask. She starts crying and falls to her knees.

"I can't get him out," she says. "He's in here. He's in me. He *is* me."

"No, Dara," I say, shaking my head. "He's *not*."

"But I can't get him out," Dara says. "He'll take over again. I feel him. He's too strong! I'm not enough. I'm so..." Dara starts to shake.

"No, no," I say. "They're lies. All lies."

With Dara's shoulders bare, I realize that I can see all the witch symbols tattooed to her body. *Ugly* stares at me right in the middle of her forehead. "You're not ugly," I say. "You're *beautiful*." I push my hand to the symbol, and when I take it away, it's gone as though it had never been. "You're not alone, you are *loved*. You're not worthless, you are *full of worth*. You are not blind, you are *true-sighted*. You're not despicable, you are *lovable*. You're not incompetent; you are *able*. You are not sickly in agony; you are *whole and well*. You are not dead, you are *alive*."

All of Dara's tattoos melt away. Her face flushes with color in a way I've never seen in her before, but her eyes are still clouded in worry.

"Fight," I say. "Fight him. Don't believe his lies. Push him out!"

"Hyuh - ack!" Dara coughs as she falls forward, gasping and wheezing as the first gloopy spittle comes up. Then more, and with one giant heave, the caterpillar comes up, deposited in a pool of gloopy vomit.

I hug Dara. I hug her so tightly that I wonder if I will ever let go, or whether she can even breathe, but I don't care.

"*So what!*" Notso cries, standing before us now in the form he had from my vision - a gloopy darkness in the shape of a man. "*I can anchor myself to this realm with any of my followers. There are many, and there will be many more! They will fill the whole realm until I have subdued all to my will. No one will be able to stop me!*"

"Sunny," I say, realizing I have no actual idea what to do. And then, to my surprise, there are several flashes of light, and with them several people appear – people who look young, about my age, but they seem to glow with the light I usually only see in the globes inside people in my other sight.

"You are not welcome in this realm," a boy says. "We are here to return you to your own."

"Ayda," Aden says. "I know him." As I look at the boy and then around at the rest of these glowing people, I realize they all look familiar to me, too.

"Rollo?" Aden asks.

Rollo smiles. "And Cinda, Torwin, Clyde, Gola, Horn, Aven, Vye, and Domo," he says.

"Notso," Cinda says in a loud commanding voice, "we were chosen as sacrifices to take back that which was stolen. Your followers slew us before we could complete our mission. So we are here now to oppose you and eject you from this realm."

The past centenaries surround Notso in a circle and combine their hands so that the light coming from them grows and grows. Notso, meanwhile, begins to shriek and bellow all the louder as the light reaches its zenith, and then the sounds stop abruptly. The glow begins to fade, and once I can see the center of the circle again, he is no longer there.

"The Dastardly Wyrm is banished!" Sorru cries, bringing shouts of joy and ululation from the Wildrians. "I proclaim a feast at our stronghold in the mountains! Warriors of the Centenary - come, join us!"

The great warriors clad in light turn now with faces unmoved.

"We cannot," Rollo says. "We are the protectors of this realm, and we are from this place, but we now reside afar in the realm Indescribable. Someday you will join the feast there, and we will celebrate together. Sandor will sit at the head of that table, and he will speak of this day and praise those who followed him and did his will."

With that, Rollo and the others lift off the ground to float weightlessly into the air. The glimmering light about them grows and grows.

"Wait!" I cry, feeling drawn to them. But they do not wait, and in another moment they are gone, and I am left behind and filled with an ache that I don't understand.

"Ayda," Aden calls. "You're here. You're still here. Stay here with us."

Chapter 37

The Wildrian stronghold is more than I could have imagined, made up of tunnels dug through limestone in the mountains, and it reminds me a great deal of their home back in Wildria. The feast, too, is larger than I would have suspected from warriors so far removed from their island nation.

The food comes out in a parade - roasted meat on spits carried on shields with cooked vegetables garnished around it. Games are set up, and conversation roars among the warriors about impossible shots made during the battle, surviving hexes, and other daring feats.

"Eat! Eat!" Sorru commands, heaping a pile of cooked meat and vegetables in front of me. "Celebrate! Celebrate the victory!" Warily I lift the leg of some game bird to my mouth and eat. I take another bit and the juices run down my throat. I begin to cry again, and it doesn't seem like a thing I can help, so I go out of the caves into the night air and eat my food alone.

Once I finish, I feel too tired to celebrate, so I climb up a ladder etched into the stone wall and crawl through an entrance into the dark dwelling above the chaos and celebration below. And there I find myself an empty bed on which to lie down and close my eyes.

I sleep. I dream. And there in my dreams, I find Sunny walking along the side of a wheat field in what looks like Kern.

"Ayda," Sunny says.

"Sunny?"

Sunny smiles.

"You died," I say. "You're dead."

"Do I look dead?" Sunny asks.

I shake my head.

"Life is my word," Sunny says. "I spoke it long ago, but it is still mine. It comes from me and is part of me."

"I was just surprised. I mean, I watched you die," I say somberly. "You died to get the words back."

"Yes." Sunny says. "It was my choice to die, my choice to take the sacrifice upon myself – just like you made a choice. See, that choice is the beginning. And now you have another choice – will you walk with me?"

"Walk with you?" I ask.

"Walk with me," Sunny says.

"...But, where will we go?" I ask.

"Many places," Sunny says. "There are many to invite, many who are still bound by Notso's lies, many who need the freedom of my words."

"I - yes," I say. "I was, I-"

"You were afraid that everything was over," Sunny says. "One adventure ends, and another begins. When you walk with me, they will never end."

"And what am *I* supposed to do?" I ask. "How do I get the people to join us?"

"Share the words," Sunny says. "Destroy the lies of the enemy. Even though he is gone for now, the chains he forged remain, and those who wear them don't remember what it was like to be free. So you must show them, even when they cling to their bondage, even when they hate and despise you. So be careful. Our enemy is crafty. He will bind you back in his lies if he can."

"And you'll be with me?" I ask. "I mean, you won't be with me like you were on our journey? Physically?"

"I'm always closer than you think," Sunny says. "If my words are with you, I am with you."

"....uh, right," I say, nodding.

"Do you trust me, Ayda?"

"...*Yes*," I say, nodding as another tear comes to my eyes.

"Then trust me now," Sunny says.

"Alright," I say. "I guess there's a lot to do."

"I guess there is," Sunny says, still running his hand through the grains of wheat. "Don't forget, anytime you talk to me, I'll hear."

"Wait!" I say.

"That's not the right phrase, Ayda," Sunny says as the vision fades. "It's *just* wait." And with one last smile, Sunny is gone.

When I wake up, I climb down from the sleeping quarters and find the wreckage of the celebration everywhere – broken chairs, dirty shields and uneaten food in strange places, people sleeping on the floor. I carefully make my way through it all and follow the glow of purple and orange light. When I make it outside I find the mountains and the sky painted with it. And there, on a lookout's ledge, I find Dara staring off into this view. I climb up to the ledge then and I settle down next to her.

"Well," I say.

"Well," Dara says.

"....I'm sorry." She doesn't continue, just keeps her eyes focused on the mountains.

"Well, I'm not," I say. "I thought I was going to lose you, and you're here."

"Am I?" Dara asks. "I mean, I guess I am, but I don't know who I am anymore."

"I know who you are," I say.

Dara nods.

"Maybe I want to be that person," Dara says, "but...I don't know if I can be..."

"Well, I know one thing," I say. "I know that you're my friend. For now, can that be enough?"

Dara nods again.

"I'm going to be leaving here soon," I say. "Sunny has more for me to do."

Dara smirks. "Of *course* he does."

"...And, would you like to come with me?" I ask.

Slowly Dara nods. Then she shoots me a look and says, "Don't tell me you're going to invite Naru, too."

"What? We need a navigator," I say.

"No – *you* need a navigator. You half circled the Crater before you went in."

"Because *Naru* showed me the way," I say back, laughing. I stand up. "Come on. Let's go get the others."

I go back inside and find Aden bunking near Naru and gently shake my brother awake. "What?" he asks.

"It's time to go," I say.

Aden wipes his eyes and sits up. Naru hangs down from the bunk above and says, "Maybe you could use a navigator."

"Maybe I could," I say.

"And Nina, she's a good person to have along too," Naru says.

"So she is," I say, smiling.

"But where are we going?" Aden asks.

"On a new adventure," I say. "Or at least that's what Sunny says."

"A new – *what?*" Aden asks. "But Sunny, he's...*dead.*"

"No Aden," I say with a laugh, "he's not dead. Sunny's very much alive..."